BOOTS & TWISTERS

UGLY STICK SALOON BOOK #11

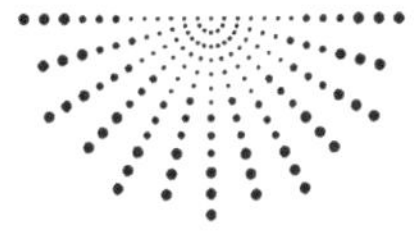

MYLA JACKSON

TWISTED PAGE INC

BOOTS & TWISTERS

UGLY STICK SALOON SERIES #11

New York Times & USA Today
Bestselling Author

ELLE JAMES

writing as

MYLA JACKSON

EBOOK ISBN: 978-1-62695-111-2

PRINT ISBN: 978-1-62695-112-9

This book is dedicated to proud, hardy men and women who've survived the tragedy and destruction of tornadoes and have the courage to rebuild and start over.

$\mathcal{L}$ucky Albright had been driving all day and she still wasn't out of Texas. Worse, she had no idea where she was. With her gas gauge on empty, her stomach gnawing a hole clean through to her backside, and her wallet bone dry of remedying either of her first two issues, she pulled into the parking lot of the only building she'd seen since the last small town of Hole in the Wall. Maybe, just maybe, someone inside could point her to the nearest homeless shelter.

Because that was what she was.

Homeless.

She reached up to swipe at the ready tears, cursing herself for shedding even one when the people of Comfort, Texas, had been anything but a comfort to her. Hell, they'd run her out of town like an unwanted stray dog. All she'd been looking for was a quiet place to call her home. And they'd kicked her out after a series of unfortunate events that hadn't been her fault at all.

She could still picture the mayor of Comfort along with

over half the town loading her meager belongings into her truck.

"Get out of town and stay out of town," the mayor had said. "In fact, get the hell out of Texas. Your kind is not wanted anywhere near the great Lone Star State."

Her kind?

With townsfolk lined up along the street, blocking her return to city limits, she had felt like she was part of a cartoon or a reality show about being punked. Surely this wasn't happening to her. She had every right to be in that town. Never in her life had she committed a crime, she followed rules, she was an upstanding citizen.

So she'd had a run of bad luck. It wasn't her fault Mitsy Grumbal's dog tangled with a skunk, Joe Sarli wrecked into the side of one of their precious historic buildings, Raymond Rausch's cow had gotten loose and trampled the flowers around the town square, or the public library had burned down. But somehow, she'd been the one closest to the incidents and she'd taken the blame. Taken wasn't exactly the term she'd use. Assigned was closer to reality.

As she drove through the parking lot packed with a Saturday night crowd, the tears blurred her eyes, but she refused to shed even one more. Before she could find a place to pull in, her engine sputtered and died. Her beat-up pickup drifted to a stop behind four large, shiny new trucks.

Empty.

Lucky leaned her head on the steering wheel, fighting back more tears. "Fuck this!" she yelled, slamming her palm against the dash. "I'm an Albright. Albrights don't give up and they sure as shootin' don't cry." She unbuckled her seat belt, climbed down from the truck, tucked her hair up into her cowboy hat and strode for the front door of the building, glancing up at the crooked sign hanging overhead.

Ugly Stick Saloon.

Figured. She could use a beer about now, but she didn't have the money to buy one, much less a gallon of gas to get her into the next town. All she could hope for was to find work washing dishes, scrubbing toilets or, if her luck changed, landing a job with a rancher who needed a ranch hand. One who would give her a lift to the ranch until she could afford to put gas in her truck and bring it with her.

Music pulsed through the corrugated tin walls of the building. As Lucky stepped through the front entrance, she could hear the excited screams of the women inside.

A large gender-ambiguous person stood guard just inside the door, blocking her entrance. "Sorry, mister, it's Ladies Night. No men allowed."

Lucky didn't mind when people mistook her for a man. She was taller than most women and slender, more athletic than curvy. And she liked to wear men's jeans, chambray shirts and cowboy boots. The horses and cows she preferred to work with didn't care what she wore or how she wore it.

But right at that moment, she needed to get inside and find help. Either that or stay the night in her truck, blocking the four larger trucks in their parking spaces.

"Suits me just fine." She swept off the cowboy hat and let her long sandy-blond hair fall down about her shoulders. That too would have been cut short, but she hadn't had time or the spare cash to get it cut in the past couple months and it grew like hay in a warm summer rain.

The bouncer's eyes narrowed and gave her a swift appraising once-over before nodding. "There's a five-dollar cover charge to get in tonight." A meaty hand came out, palm up.

Crap. If she'd had five bucks, she wouldn't be out of gas at this point. She'd have bought a gallon in Hole in the Wall instead of risking another fifteen miles to Temptation. "Look, my truck...stalled out in the parking lot. I need to speak with the owner."

"Sorry, Audrey Anderson is busy."

Feeling more desperate by the second, Lucky put on her best poker face and insisted, "I need to speak with Ms. Anderson."

The bouncer crossed beefy arms over a broad chest. "Unless you pay the cover charge, you ain't gettin' in."

Defeated, Lucky trudged back to her truck. She couldn't leave it in the middle of the parking lot, blocking other vehicles from getting out. She put it in neutral and, rounded to the back and leaned with all her might against the tailgate. The heavy vehicle barely moved an inch.

Throwing all the anger and frustration she'd lived with over the past two years into her next push, she got the truck rolling. Grunting and pushing, she plowed her feet into the gravel and the vehicle moved faster.

Until that moment, Lucky hadn't noticed the slight slope leading to the far end of the parking lot, the line of trucks and the drainage ditch beyond.

Once the truck was in motion, she glanced up and froze momentarily.

The truck was now rolling at a good clip and headed straight for a bright red pickup, with a shiny paint job and a license plate that read USS1.

Lucky dug her heels into the gravel and leaned back, holding on to the bumper, but it did little slow the momentum, her worn boot heels kicking up lines of dust behind her.

"No," she said out loud, visions of the charred remains of the Comfort Public Library flooding her head. "Not again." She willed the strength of a bulldozer into her back and tried again to slow the vehicle.

It rolled faster, until it slammed into the back of the pretty red truck, forcing its front wheels over the edge of the embankment, where it teetered for a moment. Gravity and the weight of Lucky's truck gave it an added *oomph*, and it slid down into the drainage ditch below.

Her own truck followed the red truck into the ditch, metal crunching metal.

Catching herself before she too pitched over the edge, Lucky teetered on the embankment, staring down at the wreckage, her heart sinking into her boots.

"Holy shit."

Why was it when she thought things were really bad they got worse? The phrase *it only goes up from here* never entered her realm of possibilities.

She stood for a long time, staring at the trucks in the ditch, wondering how she'd talk her way out of this one.

"Fuck, Audrey's gonna be pissed," a voice said beside her. A pretty blonde stood with glazed eyes and a tight skirt just behind Lucky, swaying slightly.

"Yup. Audrey loves that truck. Almost as much as she loves her red boots," an equally pretty brunette said.

"I didn't mean for it to happen. It was an accident."

"Mister, you got some 'splainin' to do." The blonde hiccuped, pressed a hand to her lips and stared at the brunette, her eyes rounded and dancing with amusement.

The brunette with the big brown eyes giggled. "Shh. Mona, you're swayin'."

Mona hiccuped and pointed at the brunette. "Don't think you're so cool, Bunny. You're swayin' too."

They hugged each other, falling to the ground giggling.

Lucky's gut twisted. "Please tell me that truck didn't belong to Audrey Anderson, the owner of the Ugly Stick Saloon."

The women giggled more, rolling on the ground, Mona aware enough to say, "Okay, we won't tell you. Shh, Bunny, it's a secret."

"Fuck secrets." Bunny laughed again, her eyes filling with tears of senseless, uncontrollable mirth. "Jackson just bought her that truck to match her favorite boots."

"Do you suppose you could go back into the Ugly Stick Saloon and ask her to come outside?" Lucky asked, biting back her frustration at the two women's staggering inebriation.

"Sure," Mona said. "Wanna see her face when she realizes that's her truck in the ditch."

"Me too. Wait, where's *my* truck?" Bunny asked.

"You rode with me, silly. Besides, you don't own a truck."

"That's right." Bunny giggled.

"Do you two mind getting Audrey?" Lucky reminded them.

"Going," Mona responded. "Come on. Maybe we can see Cory dance again."

Lucky followed the two ladies to the door.

"Greta Sue, we're back," Mona sang and showed the bouncer the ink stamp on her wrist.

Bunny did the same and the bouncer allowed them inside, while Lucky received an eat-shit-and-die-because-you're-not-getting-inside-without-the-requisite-cover-charge look.

Greta Sue. Hell, who knew she was female?

Lucky held her breath as Greta Sue pointed at her, her gaze narrowing, warning her not to make any sudden moves.

Lucky waited, the acids in her empty stomach churning, eating a hole through the lining. What would she say to the owner of the Ugly Stick? Would she be like her bouncer, large, bulky and friggin' scary? Would she slam her into the ground with one thick stump of a fist and leave her there to die?

She'd considered death as an alternative, but Lucky had one problem with that…she liked living.

The scent of beer and grilled burgers drifted toward her from inside the bar and she swayed with hunger, not having eaten since the night before. She truly was in hell.

Greta Sue closed the door to the stomach-churning smells, leaving Lucky out in the dark. A minute passed, then two. Had the two ladies forgotten? As plastered as they were, that could have been the case.

Seven minutes passed before Lucky came to the sad conclusion the ladies had either gotten lost in the crowd, or forgotten. From all the whooping and hollering going on inside, Lucky guessed it was the latter.

She wondered if there was a rear entrance. If she could at least sneak inside and find Audrey, she could break the bad news and hopefully avoid going to jail. She rounded the tin building that vibrated with the sound of the sexy music and screams from the crowd. A door at the back opened and a woman stepped out carrying a bag of trash. She propped the door to keep it from shutting, then set off for the large trash bin set away from the building.

Her heart hammering, Lucky saw her break and took it. She ran for the door, careful not to make too much noise and ducked inside. The back of the building had a hallway with a room off to the left and another to the right. Footsteps on the porch behind her made her turn left. Her back to the room, she peeked out into the hallway, waiting for the person to pass by.

"Hey, buddy, you dancin' tonight?" a male voice said behind her. "Or are you lookin' for the poker game?"

Lucky spun, her cheeks burning and her jaw dropped. A truly beautiful man with long blond hair stood in front of her, wearing nothing but a G-string and chaps. He stuck out his hand. "Cory McBride."

"Lucky Albright," she said automatically.

"Nice to meet you. So what is it? Poker or dance?" He waved toward the other men in various states of undress. All equally as handsome as the man in front of her. Holy hell, they were strippers!

Lucky swallowed hard to ease her dry throat. "Poker," she eked out.

"Across the hall." Cory opened the door and pointed at another door.

"Thanks," she said.

"Don't you let them eat you alive."

Lucky glanced down the hallway. The coast was clear and she stepped out When the door didn't close behind her, she glanced back at the man.

He nodded. "That's the one. Go on in."

It was go in or admit she wasn't there for either dancing or poker.

She chose the door to the right and walked in, turning to close it behind her.

A light glowed from around an inside corner.

"That you, Audrey?" a voice called out.

Lucky didn't answer, praying they'd think the door opened and closed and no one had actually entered.

"Guess it wasn't Audrey," the voice said. "I'm going for a refill on our pitcher of beer. Anyone have an objection to Budweiser? Jackson, Nick, Isaac?"

"Bring me back one of those horny women," one man called out. "And while you're at it get one for yourself. You've been too uptight lately. You really need a wife."

The others chuckled.

The voice moving nearer responded with, "I'm not ready to be shackled to someone who doesn't know a horse shoe from a stiletto."

"What you need is a good old-fashioned cowgirl. Boots, jeans, hat and all. No nonsense, no frills."

"That's exactly what I need, Jackson," the voice said.

"One who can ride a horse, drive a tractor and stay up all night with a sick cow," the one called Jackson added.

"You don't need a wife, you need a ranch hand."

"Nick, that's all well and good, but what would he do for sex?" Jackson asked.

The voice moving closer responded, "I can get that in the next county. There's a widow there who's more than happy to accommodate. No commitment required."

"Ah, that gets old."

"Hasn't yet."

"We should fix him up with someone local," Nick said.

"Got any ideas?" Jackson asked.

"The man's been picky all his life. Hasn't dated the same woman more than twice."

"All I ask is a woman who's faithful, doesn't nag, loves me and all my faults and doesn't care if I track mud on the floor." The voice sounded right next to Lucky.

One of the men chortled. "You just described my dog."

Lucky agreed, the man needed a dog, not a woman.

The man headed her way snorted. "Am I askin' too much?"

Yes. She bet he wasn't all that perfect, yet he was expecting perfection in a woman. *Jerk.*

"Yeah, big brother. When you find one like that, let me know."

"Hell, if you're nice to me, I might even share her with you. After all, what are brothers for?"

"Share, hell! I might arm wrestle you for her."

The man thought he could share a woman with his brother? What kind of asshole was he? It was as if the woman would have no say in the matter. No wonder he wasn't married. With his attitude, what woman would have him?

"Since I'm not likely to find one out in the crowd tonight, don't worry. You won't get your ass kicked at the arm wrestling."

"I hope your arm wrestling is better than your poker skills."

The men laughed while Lucky glanced around, looking for a place to hide and finding none. She whipped off her hat, letting her hair fall down around her shoulders. Surely the man wouldn't be threatened by a girl and throw a punch at her.

When the man rounded the corner, he stopped short, all his six-foot something, broad-shouldered, dark-haired gorgeousness. "What the hell?"

"You say something, Trent?" Jackson's deep voice called out.

Lucky pleaded with her eyes, pressing a finger to her lips. Holy hell, the man in front of her should have been on the other side of the hallway preparing to strip. He certainly had the body for it. And with his ego the size of Texas, he could pull it off.

Trent's eyes narrowed and he hesitated before replying, "No, just stubbed my toe." His gaze traveled the length of her.

"There's a light switch on the wall by the door," Isaac said.

"I'm okay, just a little unlucky. However, I have high hopes of getting luckier." His mouth curved upward in a smooth, sexy grin.

Lucky's heart beat faster and her knees wobbled. If she thought he was good looking before the smile…wow. And she usually didn't get all weak-kneed around men, seeing them as competition, not the prize.

"*We* hope your lousy luck holds true through the rest of the hands."

A rumble of chuckles sounded from the men out of sight.

Trent motioned toward the door with the empty plastic pitcher in his hand.

Lucky opened it slowly, peeked out and sighed when she'd determined that the door across the hallway was closed and the hallway itself was empty. She stepped out and turned around to face Trent so fast she knocked the pitcher from his hand. It skidded across the floor to the other side.

They both bent to pick it up at the same time.

Lucky reached it first, grabbed and jerked upright, her skull colliding with his nose.

"Damn!" Trent exclaimed.

Lucky's head smarted and she swayed at the pain. When she could focus her gaze on him, her heart sank to her wobbly knees.

Trent clutched his nose, his eyes watering, blood trickling down his chin.

"Oh hell. Did I do that?" Her belly clenched. If she could find a way to screw things up, she did. With a frantic glance around the empty hallway, she despaired of finding a towel to stem the flow of blood. With a desperate jerk, she pulled her shirt off her back, thankful she'd worn a tank top beneath the chambray. She held the garment up to his face. "Move your hands," she commanded.

He did, the blood dripping onto her shirt. She pressed the fabric to his nose gently. "I'm sorry. I didn't mean to hurt you. Are you okay?" she asked, staring into the most beautiful dark chocolate eyes she'd ever seen. She could fall right into those and get lost forever. Good grief! She'd never been this mesmerized by a man before. Ever.

Her pulse hammering against her ears, she pulled the shirt away from his nose. "It's already stopped bleeding."

"Good." He flung the shirt to the side, grabbed both of her wrists and pinned them to the wall above her head. "Perhaps you could tell me why you were hiding in the poker room, and why you were back here where only employees are allowed. I don't think I've seen you working here before." He pinned her body to the wall with his, not giving her room to raise her knee fast and hard enough to hit him where it counted.

She squirmed, fighting against his strong hold, the heat of his body against hers doing funny things to her insides. It had been a long time since a man had bested her and it infuriated her as well as sparked something in her that she'd thought long dead.

Lust.

And damned if he didn't smell good. Like saddle leather and a subtle aftershave. She loved the smell of leather and aftershave. It made her feel all girlie. With a gasp, she fought harder. "Let go of me. I was looking for Audrey Anderson."

"If you're here to rob her, you'll have to go through everyone else in the place to get to her." His grip tightened.

"I'm not here to rob Audrey or anyone else."

"Then what do you want with her?"

"None of your business."

"You made it my business when you snuck into our poker game."

Lucky chewed on her lip, hating that he held her so securely and hating even more that *her* body was reacting to *his* leaning against hers. "I have something to tell her."

"Tell me and I'll pass it on to her."

She straightened, her lips pressing into a tight line. She didn't like being manhandled—even if he smelled good enough to lick—and worse, she didn't want to confess her crime to this man. "I'll tell her what I came to say when I see her."

"Tell you what...I'll let the bouncer decide."

Lucky's eyes widened. As much as she disliked being detained by this man, the bouncer was a thousand times scarier. "I need to see Audrey. It's very important. And the bouncer wouldn't let me."

"Greta Sue won't let you? Why?"

"Because..." She searched for a good reason other than the truth. Shame made her cheeks burn. She didn't want to admit she was broke and couldn't afford the cover charge to get in. "Because. Damn it!"

"Not good enough."

Anger, shame, desperation roiled up and exploded. "I couldn't pay the cover charge to get in the front door. There! Are you satisfied?" Her bottom lip trembled and she bit into it to keep it steady. She'd never been down and out before in her life and it galled her no end. "Look, just let me talk to her and I'll leave as soon as I can." She'd have to walk, but she'd leave just to get away from the man and the way he made her heart pound like horses hooves on hard-packed dirt in an all-out gallop.

"Look, I'm feeling generous tonight. I'll get you that meeting with Audrey."

Hope surged, along with the dread of having to tell the owner of the bar she'd run her truck into a ditch. "You will?"

He nodded. "On one condition."

Her brows narrowed. She knew it was too good to be true. People always wanted something. Nothing ever came for free, and normally she was just fine with that, except now. She was broke. "What condition?"

"One kiss." His gaze shifted to her lips.

She struggled against his hold on her hands. "No."

He let go of one hand and dragged her toward the rear exit with the other.

She dug in her boot heels but got no traction from the smooth wood floors. He out-weighed her, out-muscled her and she could do nothing to stop him. Stubborn resignation set in. What good did it do to fight? He refused to relent and she was going nowhere. Lucky quit fighting and followed.

He opened the door and waved a hand toward the back parking area. "I suggest you take it up with Greta Sue at the front entrance."

Lucky assumed that because she hadn't fought him the last few steps, he thought she'd go willingly. When he let go of her hand, she let her shoulders sag as if defeated, but she was far from it.

"You're missing your chance to meet Audrey." His brows rose invitingly. "It won't cost you much. Just one little kiss."

Her chin tipped up. "When I kiss a man, it's because I want to, not because I need a favor. And frankly, I find nothing kissable about you." Her gaze traveled his length from tip to toe and heat flared, belying her words. There were far too many kissable things about this man, except for his inflated ego and his unrealistic views on a perfect woman. "Now, if you'll excuse me."

He stepped back to let her pass.

She stuck out her hand, offering to shake his. Hoping he'd take it so that she could use the one trick she knew to subdue a randy cowboy. When he set his hand in hers, she twisted and yanked his hand up behind his back and between his shoulder blades, then planted her boot on his cute ass and shoved him through the doorway, slamming it shut behind him.

She spun so fast she almost fell. Then she ran in the opposite direction, hoping to get lost in the crowd before tall, dark and arrogant could catch up with her. Then maybe she'd find Audrey and break the bad news to her.

The door behind her slammed open, but she didn't turn to see who was there, knowing she only had seconds to make good her escape.

Coming from behind the bar, Lucky spied the bartender, a pretty woman with auburn hair, wearing black leather like she meant it.

"Excuse me," Lucky shouted over the rabid crowd of screaming women.

A man danced on the stage. One with long blond hair and a killer body dressed in nothing but a G-string.

Lucky recognized him as the man she'd met in the

back. Cory, he'd said was his name. His body was perfect, one she'd love to stay and watch, if only she wasn't facing a huge bill to have the owner's truck fixed with money she didn't have. How did she manage to get in situations like this?

The bartender slapped five mugs of beer onto a tray before she turned to Lucky. "What can I get you?" she asked.

"Audrey Anderson?"

The bartender nodded toward the stage where a woman introduced the blond-haired man to the audience as Cory McBride. "She's the emcee, right now."

Lucky groaned. To get to her, she had to wade through tightly packed women who appeared to have staked their claims on their own pieces of the floor, unwilling to let anyone else get closer. They fought to place bills in the man's G-string and get their opportunity to grope.

Lucky snorted. This was not the scene for her. She wanted a man who didn't have to dance for a living. One who worked with animals. Feeling more comfortable around animals than people, Lucky was far out of her element in the packed barroom. But it couldn't be helped. She had to get to Audrey and let her know what had happened.

Trying not to step on anyone, she pushed her way through the crowd, taking elbows to the gut, her boots stomped on by other cowboy boots and some stilettos. All the while she kept a watch out for the bouncer.

The tighter the bodies pushed up against her, the shallower her breathing became. She'd never been good in tight places. Claustrophobia, her daddy had called it. Her heart pattered against her ribs, and her palms sweat. A moment before Lucky would have passed out, the pretty strawberry blonde wearing a pair of short shorts and red cowboy boots stepped down from the stage.

"Are you all right?" she asked, touching Lucky's arm.

Her vision graying around the edges, Lucky swayed and didn't see the bouncer until she grabbed her from behind. "How'd you get in here?" she demanded.

"Greta Sue," the bar owner said. "She's not well. Let's get her out of this crush."

"I'll get her out. All the way out of the building. Plenty of air to breathe outside. She didn't pay the cover charge."

The strawberry blonde smiled. "It's okay. I'll cover for her this time."

"But, Ms. Anderson, she snuck in somehow. That's trespassin'."

"It's okay. I'm sure she has a good reason." Ms. Anderson led her to the edge of the jostling crowd and already Lucky could breathe better.

Lucky held her breath as Greta Sue pointed at her, her gaze narrowing, warning her not to make any sudden moves.

The strawberry blonde smiled and held out a hand to Lucky. "I'm Audrey Anderson, owner of the Ugly Stick Saloon. How may I help you?"

Her voice was warm, friendly and so likable it made Lucky want the floor to swallow her whole. Why couldn't Audrey Anderson have been old, ugly and mean-spirited? Breaking the bad news to this sweet woman made her feel even more of a heel.

Lucky took her hand and shook it, cringing inwardly, at a loss as to how to explain how she'd managed to wreck both her own truck and that of the pretty woman standing in front of her with the friendly smile and the firm handshake.

She cleared her throat and blurted, "I have some bad news."

Audrey's brows knit and she stepped closer. "Jackson. Is he all right?"

Lucky frowned. "Who's Jackson?"

"My boyfriend. I assumed the bad news was about him. Are you telling me it's not?"

With a shake of her head, Lucky waved her hand toward the doorway. "It's best I show you."

Greta Sue gave Lucky the stink-eye. "You hurt one hair on Ms. Anderson's head..." Audrey Anderson had her share of folks looking out for her. A stab of longing tugged at Lucky's heart. It would be nice to be loved that much by so many people.

Lucky raised her hands in surrender. "I'm not going to hurt her."

"Damn right you're not." Greta Sue followed them out the door. "I'm coming with you."

Great. More witnesses to Lucky's destruction and mortification.

"Tell me what happened." Audrey walked beside Lucky, her feet moving briskly in the night air, her bright red cowboy boots crunching gravel.

"I stalled out in the parking lot and didn't have any help moving my truck, so I pushed it. And well..." Lucky stopped where Audrey's red truck used to be parked.

The strawberry blonde's brows dipped together. Her gaze moved from the empty spot to glance around the parking lot. "Didn't I park my truck here? For that matter, I don't see it anywhere."

Lucky bit down on her lower lip, touched the Ugly Stick owner's arm and pointed to the ditch. "It's in there."

Audrey stepped up to the edge of the embankment and

stared down at the shapes of the two trucks wedged into the ditch at angles. As recognition dawned, she gasped. "That's my new truck!"

TRENT COULDN'T BELIEVE a girl had bested him. Isaac, Nick and Jackson would all have laughed had they witnessed his humiliation. Strange that the embarrassment and fact that he'd been tricked only made him that much more determined to get that kiss.

No sooner had he been shoved out the door, he turned, caught the door before it closed and stormed back inside, only to see the tall, slender, cool drink of cowgirl water slip into the darkness of the bar. Well, hell. It was Ladies Night and Audrey had given them strict instructions to limit their movements to the employee-only area of the bar or risk being pinched, kissed, squeezed and fondled by a couple hundred horny women.

Trent debated following her, but he'd heard of how Jackson had been stripped to his skivvies once on Ladies Night and he had no desire to be exposed in such a way.

So he didn't get his kiss. What harm could one more woman add to a room full of raging estrogen?

He returned to the poker game and settled in, his mind on the cowgirl, not his hand. No sooner had Jackson dealt the cards, Nick got a call to tow two trucks.

"Audrey, is that you?" Nick asked.

Jackson frowned. "Trouble?"

"Two trucks in the ditch out front." Nick tossed his cards on the table and rose. "I'll be right there."

"Two trucks?" Trent's brother, Isaac, asked. "Things must be hoppin' on Ladies Night."

"What's going on? The strippers try to make a run for

it?" Trent joked, wondering if the woman he'd let go into the bar had anything to do with the trucks in the ditch. A jab of guilt twisted in his belly. He should have let Audrey know she'd had a trespasser.

"Sorry, guys," Nick said. "You're welcome to stay and play, but I've got work to do. Seems Audrey's was one of the trucks that got knocked into the ditch."

"Audrey's?" Jackson jumped to his feet. "She wasn't in it, was she?" Jackson checked his cell phone. "Fuck. I had my ringer off. Audrey's been tryin' to get a hold of me. She called three times." He punched the screen on his phone and held it to his ear.

"No, someone else's vehicle pushed it into the ditch. Come on. Let's check it out. I could use a hand getting them out."

"Maybe we should all go check it out." Trent tossed his hand onto the table and pushed to his feet.

"I guess we're all going, since it's kind of hard to play one-handed poker." Isaac stood and stretched. "Besides, with a bunch of horny women leaving the Ugly Stick, we might get lucky tonight."

"I've been in the middle of that mob before. Scared the jitters out of me," Jackson admitted. "Let's go 'round the back to the front and find Greta Sue. She can run inter-ference."

"She can't guard us all. Frankly, I don't want her to. I'll take my chances with the ladies." Isaac rubbed his hands together. "I could use a little distraction after having my butt kicked at poker."

"Must be the Jameson luck," Nick said.

Isaac chuckled. "Remind me not to play poker with Jackson and Nick. I'm completely out of my league here."

"We both are." Trent jerked his head toward the door. "Come on."

Jackson feathered through the handful of bills he collected from the table and stuffed them in his pocket. "You two are more than welcome to come throw money at us anytime."

Nick headed for his tow truck he'd parked at the rear of the building. Tonight was a full moon. People always got crazy at the full moon. Otherwise, the mechanic would have ridden his motorcycle.

Jackson climbed into the passenger seat of the tow truck's cab.

Trent and Isaac slowly walked around the building.

"Did you put that ad in the paper for a ranch hand?" Isaac asked.

Trent shook his head. "I put a flyer up at the feed store and here at the Ugly Stick."

"I took a whack at an ad for the newspaper, we'll see what we can get. We have more work than we can shake a stick at and no relief until Dusty gets back."

Dusty, their ranch foreman, was out recuperating from knee replacement after having been thrown one too many times by Thunder, the meanest horse they had.

"Yeah, cattle to round up, horses to train and pastures to cut. Should have hired someone a month ago."

"Whose idea was it anyway for us to do our own ranchin'? We have the money to pay someone else," Trent reminded Isaac.

"I can hear Dad's voice in my head. *You're gettin' too big for your britches, boy.*" Isaac dug his thumbs in his belt loops and rocked back on his boot heels with a deep scowl, just like their father wore when he was delivering a lecture on the sins of laziness. Isaac's frown turned around and he grinned.

Trent didn't. Their taciturn father had backhanded him more than once, and he'd sworn never to return to the Triple J Ranch outside of Temptation, Texas. He hadn't come back until he'd gotten news from his brother that Old John Jameson had died of a heart attack, leaving his two-thousand-acre spread to his boys.

If he'd had his way, Trent would have sold the ranch and given the proceeds to the Wounded Warriors organization or some other worthy cause. But Isaac hadn't wanted to give it up. He'd felt some sort of connection to the place.

Hell, he'd been their father's favorite and could do no wrong. The ranch probably held *good* memories for him.

Now they both lived there and worked the ranch with their own hands. Although Trent had never wanted to keep the ranch, he'd never been closer to his brother, and he was starting to work out his anger toward his father. But it was a struggle to keep the ranch going when he had full-time commitments as an oil rig architect. And the time spent ranching had given him a little more understanding and grudging respect for his late father.

Isaac had insisted they do the work themselves, telling him it would keep them humble when their bank accounts were overflowing and they could have anything they wanted.

Trent wasn't afraid of hard work, but they needed help to keep the ranch up. The fences alone took all their time, mending and restringing wire to keep the cattle from straying. And the horses needed exercise and training, and the hay needed cutting.

Sure, they had a foreman who ran the place when they

were away on business, but even he needed help while they were gone. Now that Dusty was out for several months, they realized just how much he'd had on his plate.

Yeah, they could use an extra pair of hands and the sooner the better.

In the meantime, his younger brother still had great expectations of finding a woman to love.

Not Trent. As a twenty-year-old, he'd thought he was in love with an older woman in her late twenties, only to find out she'd been lying to him, cheating on him with a man who could afford to buy her jewelry and fancy dates.

Since then, he hadn't trusted a woman and never went past two dates with one, determined to keep them at a distance.

"You gonna help get the trucks out of the ditch?"

"I suppose." Trent glanced at Isaac. "Go on, see if you can rescue a damsel in distress from the perils of a rowdy Ladies Night at the Ugly Stick. I'm sure one would happily take you home to tuck her into bed." His thoughts returned to the sandy-blond-haired cowgirl who'd almost busted his nose. Some of his parts, besides his nose, still throbbed at her image seared in his mind.

She hadn't been the prettiest woman he'd ever seen, but she was definitely intriguing. He wondered if she'd ever found Audrey.

He also wondered if he'd see her again. Used to being chased by women, Trent found the trespasser more than intriguing, considering she was the first woman who hadn't been too interested in kissing him.

The competitive spirit in him had flagged her as a challenge, one he'd surely overcome and grow bored with once he had caught, kissed and bedded her.

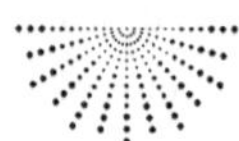

rent stared at the front parking lot of the Ugly Stick Saloon. The danged thing was chock-full. A crowd of horny, drunk women gathered around the tow truck as Nick and Jackson rigged the equipment to drag the first truck out of the ditch and back onto the parking lot.

Trent stood back, dreading the moment when the women noticed Isaac. He was the charmer. But the way they were eyeing Nick and Jackson like sides of beef on a spit had Trent shaking in his boots, ready to make a run for it.

"Look at them. Every shape, size, color and age. Women." Isaac heaved a happy sigh. "We could have our pick."

Trent shook his head. "Have you ever been to the Ugly Stick on Ladies Night?"

Isaac frowned. "Can't say that I have."

"Jackson said it's a goddamn meat fest. They get all hot and horny with the strippers and then go looking for anything with something danglin' between their legs to ride."

Isaac's brows twisted. "And that's a problem because?"

"If it's all the same to you, I'll stay right here."

"Coward." Isaac chuckled and waded into the herd and was immediately surrounded. Like carrion picking at the carcass, the women touched, pinched, fondled and threw themselves at his handsome brother.

Trent shivered.

The ladies of the Temptation Garden Club had been after him to date one of their daughters. Every time he came to town for groceries or supplies, they managed to have one on hand to shove in his direction. It was like they had radar where he was concerned.

Holy hell, and the one they'd shoved most was headed his way.

Kylie Sandell, the daughter of Mayor Sandell and Mrs. Sandell, the president of the TGC, vamped her way across the gravel parking lot, wearing stilettos, a hot pink miniskirt and a stretchy tube top that barely covered her breasts.

Trent saw her coming and dove into the pack of frothing vultures. Better to have his bones picked clean by a hundred women than to face the marriage-hungry former cheerleader with a keen focus on getting that ring she wanted on her left hand. He'd rescue his brother and get the hell out of there before Kylie got her painted claws in him. With her big blond hair and painted-on smile, she gave him the heebie-jeebies.

Once surrounded by the women in the crowd, he regretted his move immediately. He was caressed, squeezed, pawed and grabbed in places no decent woman would have done alone. In a pack, there was no telling what these lust-crazed women would sink to.

He abandoned his brother to the estrogen surge, burst through the other side of the crowd and ran down into the ditch where Jackson and Nick were hooking up Audrey's truck.

"Need a hand?" he asked.

Nick glanced up and grinned. "Look a little agitated there, Trent? Someone tweak your 'nads?"

"More than I cared for." He threw a nervous glance over his shoulder. "Have they no shame?"

"Not after one of Audrey's strippers get them going," Jackson said. "I still have scars."

"Tell you what you can do." Nick nodded toward the top of the embankment, at the other vehicle they'd already pulled out of the ditch. "If you and Isaac could push that truck out of the way, we can bring Audrey's out."

Jackson smiled. "You might get Audrey and Greta Sue to help you part the sea of estrogen."

"You sure you don't need help down here?" Trent looked up at the women eyeing him like a prize bull at an auction. "They look like they could eat me live."

"And they probably could." Jackson chuckled. "Greta Sue and Audrey will help you out."

Trent climbed the embankment, his steps slowing until he spotted the bulky form of Greta Sue standing with the petite and beautiful strawberry blonde and someone else.

Holy hell. The woman he'd cornered in the back of the bar. She wore the tank top, jeans and cowboy boots he remembered, her chambray shirt ditched somewhere with his blood on it.

Trent angled his steps toward them and stopped short

of the top of the rise. "Think we can move these people back?"

Audrey and Greta Sue glanced his way and nodded.

Greta Sue put her fingers to her lips and blew out a sharp, loud whistle.

The noisy crowd of women quieted by a few decibels and Greta shouted over the tops of their heads, "Show's over. Go home, or go back inside."

The ladies grumbled and booed Greta Sue until she blew that ear-piercing whistle again.

Audrey stepped up to the crowd. "Last round's on me and I'll get Cory to do one more encore. How 'bout it, ladies?"

As one, they shouted, "Yeehaw!" The mob turned and pushed and shoved through the front door of the Ugly Stick until the last woman disappeared inside.

Greta Sue and Audrey followed, leaving the sandy blonde standing with her hands tucked into her back pockets, the effect pushing out her breasts under the thin tank top. For all the jeans, boots and cowboy hat, the woman was beautiful in her own way. Long and lean with full yet proportional breasts.

Trent still wanted that kiss.

Isaac joined him. "I tried to get in, but Greta Sue gave me the boot. Told her I'd strip with Cory if she let me in. She said something about a riot and shoved me out the door." He glanced down at his clothes. "Well, damn. So much for pullin' an all-nighter. Didn't get a chance to get even one phone number." His clothes were askew, and he had more than one color of lipstick print on his face, shirt and chest. He even had a disturbing lipstick print on the crotch of his jeans.

"Come on." Ignoring the tall cowgirl in his peripheral

vision, Trent jerked his head toward the vehicle in the middle of the parking lot. "I could use your help pushing this truck out of the way."

When Trent reached for the handle of the driver's door the woman who'd refused to kiss him, pressed her hand to the door, keeping Trent from opening it. "What do you think you're doing?" she asked in a soft, gravelly voice.

"We need to move this hunk of junk." Trent started to open the door, but the woman leaned on it.

"That's my truck you're talking bad about," she said.

"It has to move so that they can bring the other one out." Trent frowned at her. "If it's yours, get in and drive."

She stiffened. "I can't. It won't run."

"Bad spark plugs?" Isaac asked. "Dead battery?"

She shook her head and muttered, "Ran out of gas."

Trent sighed. "Get in," he commanded.

The woman frowned then climbed into the driver's seat and held on to the steering wheel.

Trent rounded to the back of the vehicle where Isaac joined him.

"Ready?" Trent called out.

"Ready," the driver responded.

"You realize this is the truck that pushed Audrey's into the ditch, don't you?" Isaac asked as he leaned his shoulder into the rear of the truck and they both pushed.

"Yeah." Trent dug his feet into the gravel and pushed with all his might. "So?" he grunted.

The truck didn't budge.

"She's kind of pretty in the girl-next-door way. Think she'd go out with me?"

"No."

"No?" Isaac frowned. "Why not?"

Gritting his teeth, Trent hissed, "Just push, damn it."

They renewed their effort, the truck refusing to move even an inch.

"You might want to take your foot off the brake and put it in neutral," Trent called out.

"Oh sorry," she said. A sharp click and the truck rocked, the brake lights lighting up. "I'm ready."

"Let's go." Trent leaned into the truck.

Between him and Isaac, they pushed the truck to the end of the parking lot and next to Trent's.

The tall drink of spitfire water pulled the parking brake and climbed down. "Thanks."

"Let's see if we can get Audrey to let us in long enough to wash up," Isaac said.

Trent snorted. "Did you forget so soon?"

"Oh yeah, back door's locked. And even if we go in front, we won't get past Greta Sue."

"Tell me about it." The woman crossed her arms beneath her breasts, only emphasizing their lovely swell.

His cock twitching, Trent couldn't help but stare.

Isaac smiled, his gaze on her breasts as well. "If I mention I was helping Audrey, she'd let me in. I think deep down she likes me."

Trent shook his head, not at all interested in getting inside the Ugly Stick when the women in there were hungry with lust and not afraid to attack anything male. "I think I'll stay out here."

"Suit yourself," Isaac said.

"I need to talk to Audrey again," the woman said. "I'd appreciate if you could get me in too."

"Done." Isaac led the way confidently.

When the sandy blonde started to follow, Trent snagged her arm and held her back. She smelled of sunshine and the outdoors, unlike many of the women doused in perfume that reminded him of bug repellent. "Is this why you wanted in to see Audrey?" He spoke in a low voice so that his brother didn't hear.

She stared at the hand on her arm. "What do you think?"

He touched his sore nose. "I think you're trouble."

Her gaze turned stony, her lips thinning. "Let go of me."

Trent's eyes narrowed. He'd struck a nerve. What kind of trouble was she keeping to herself, besides knocking Audrey's truck into a ditch and nearly breaking his nose?

He released her arm. "Despite your propensity for bad luck, I still find myself wanting that kiss."

"Keep wantin'. You're not getting it." She spun and walked away, without glancing back.

Trent's gaze followed her all the way into the Ugly Stick.

What was it about her that made him look twice? She wasn't his usual type. Too tall, too thin and on the tomboy side.

She'd had the courage and strength to outsmart him and shove him out the door. He could admire that in a woman. And those well-rounded breasts beneath the tank top. *Mmm.* He could admire those as well. Then again, she wasn't from around Temptation or Hole in the Wall. Either that, or he hadn't noticed her. For all he knew, she was passing through. Just as well. He had too much work on the ranch to get involved, even if he still wanted a taste of those kissable lips.

He shrugged and went back to where Nick, driving the tow truck, was pulling Audrey's bright red pickup out of the ditch.

Jackson stood to one side, frowning.

"Much damage?"

"The right front fender has a big dent and one of the headlights is broken. Other than that, it's drivable."

Nick stopped once the truck was on level ground. He set the tow truck in park and climbed down. "Want me to take it to the body shop in Hole in the Wall?"

"Might as well," Jackson said. "You and Trent want to come back in for a drink first?"

"I got Lacy waiting at the house." Nick's lips stretched into a big grin. "I'd rather have a drink with her. She just texted me that she's bored and naked."

"And you're standing here?" Jackson waved at him. "Go. Bye. Worry about getting Audrey's truck to the body shop tomorrow."

"I'll park it at my shop until the morning." Nick climbed into the tow truck and drove away, pulling the red truck behind him.

"Where'd Isaac go?" Jackson asked.

Trent jerked his head toward the saloon. "To sweet talk his way past Greta Sue."

"Come on, we'll find a way in through the back door and avoid her altogether. Libby can get you a beer while I touch base with Audrey."

Trent rounded the building again. Charli, one of the waitresses, was hauling a bag full of trash through the back door.

"Here, let me." Isaac grabbed the bag and tossed it in the bin, bringing a smile to the waitress's face.

"You boys still playin' cards?" she asked.

Trent tipped his hat. "Yes, ma'am."

Charli held the door for the men.

As Trent entered, he looked around, half expecting to see the tall, sandy-blond-haired woman who wouldn't leave his thoughts. He was disappointed when he didn't see her and wondered where she'd gotten off to and if he'd see her again before he left.

Hell, he didn't even know her name.

Returning to the room where the guys had set up the card table, he waited for Jackson to enter with that beer, all the while watching the door to see if the cowgirl returned.

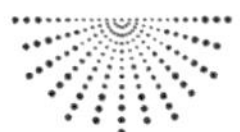

CHAPTER THREE

*L*ucky steamed at how easily Isaac talked Greta Sue into letting him into the saloon. All he had to do was tell the woman he'd helped Audrey. She wanted to call out Greta Sue on her favoritism, but the woman had let her in with Isaac. She had to talk with Audrey and apologize for knocking her vehicle into the ditch and propose a plan to pay her for the damages. Although she really had no plan with her current circumstances—homeless and jobless.

The man with pale blond hair danced on the stage, wearing nothing but a very small G-string that covered most of his impressive bulge. Every female gaze was on his glowing, naked skin, his sexy, gyrating hips and…well, his package.

Lucky dragged her gaze away from him and looked over the tops of heads to find Audrey. She finally spotted her headed through the door at the back of the building behind the bar.

Lucky pushed her way around the edges of the room

until she reached the doorway through which Audrey had disappeared.

With Greta Sue at the front door, no one stopped her as she followed Audrey into what appeared to be a storeroom filled with supplies of alcohol, paper products and plastic cups.

"Oh, Jackson, my truck," Audrey said from behind a wide stack of liquor boxes that almost reached to the ceiling of the little storage room.

"Don't worry, darlin'. It's just a truck, and at least you weren't in it," a deep, rich voice warmed the room. "Damn, you're hot tonight. Do you know what you do to me when you wear those boots?"

Lucky cleared her throat softly, hoping to get their attention.

"Oh, I know what it does to you. That's why I wear them…and lots of times…nothing else." A soft chuckle was suddenly cut off. "Jackson, I have a barroom full of people out there."

"Never stopped us before. Shed the shorts."

"Ummm. You know how to sweep a girl off her feet, don't you?" she said, her voice dripping sarcasm and sensual innuendo.

"Absolutely. Hurry the fuck up. I brought a crop."

"Oh, baby, you know how to turn me on."

Her cheeks burning, Lucky cleared her throat again. "Ms. Anderson?"

"Shh, Jackson, did you hear something?" Audrey giggled. "I can't hear past you blowing in my ear. Shh."

Lucky couldn't walk away, she had to talk to the woman whose truck she'd almost destroyed. "Ms. Anderson."

"There. I told you I heard something." Audrey called out, "Who's there?"

"Lucky Albright."

"You want me to stop?" Jackson asked.

"Hell, no. Whoever it is, you can watch, if you like." Audrey gasped. "Oh yes. Right there."

"I'll come back later," Lucky whispered, her words caught in her throat as Audrey moaned.

When her feet should have taken her backward to the door, they moved forward toward a gap in the boxes, one she could see through to the couple on the other side. Guilt slipped into wicked desire, as her glance took in the scene before her.

Audrey stood with her skirt hiked up to her waist, no sign of panties, her shirt and bra pushed up, exposing perfect, rounded breasts.

Lucky sucked in a breath and held it as Jackson lifted Audrey to sit on a box, level with his cock, jutting from his unzipped fly.

Sweet tea and grits, the man was hung like a horse and poked straight out. He pinched the tip of one of Audrey's breasts, rolling it around between his thumb and forefinger.

Lucky wondered how his fingers would feel on a naked breast. She slid her hand along her neck and down to the tip of one of her breasts, feeling it bead beneath her shirt.

Audrey gripped Jackson's cock. "I only have a few minutes. Hurry, so that I can get back to work."

"Bossy just a little?" he teased, trailing his finger down her chest to the mound of curls at the juncture of her thighs.

Lucky's hand moved the same direction, skimming over her belly to slide into the waistband of her jeans. She knew it was wrong and the naughtiness rippled over her, but she couldn't drag her gaze away from the couple making love among bottles of whiskey and beer.

"Seriously? You're going to make me beg?" Audrey planted a fist on her hip.

Jackson pulled a riding crop off a shelf behind her and tapped her thigh.

Lucky gasped, her pussy tightening. A crop? *Holy smokes.* How kinky did they get? She stepped closer to the stack of boxes, recalling how hot the man in the hallway had made her.

"So you want to play that way? Whip me, baby." Audrey lifted her thigh, exposing one cheek. "I've been so bad."

Jackson popped the crop across her naked thigh. "Say you want it."

"I want it."

"How badly?"

Lucky's breathing labored. The couple was hot. Burning, smoking, white-hot and they made her hotter. She pushed her fingers into her panties, and down between her folds. One flick and her belly clenched.

"I'm so wet," Audrey moaned. "I'm aching to feel you inside me."

"Say it."

Say it, Audrey, Lucky urged silently. *Say it.*

"Fuck me, cowboy." Audrey grabbed Jackson's hips and pulled him toward her. "Please. Do it now." She spread her legs, guiding his cock into her.

Lucky slipped a finger inside her wet channel and dragged the juices up to her clit.

As Jackson rutted into Audrey's pussy, Lucky swirled, flicked and teased herself until she panted, her body growing rigid.

Audrey cried out, her back arched and Jackson slammed into her one more time.

The fervor of their joining sent Lucky over the edge. A wave of electrical synapses rolled over her, making her gasp aloud.

Audrey's eyes widened and she stared at the gap in the boxes, straight into Lucky's eyes.

Lucky jerked her hands from her jeans and staggered backward toward the exit, heat suffusing her cheeks. Her back hit a cardboard box, and she froze, recalling the boxes stacked on wire shelves leaning precariously near the door to the storeroom.

She spun and watched in horror as the stack, shelf and all, leaned and tipped. Then, in that slow motion of impending doom, they fell.

Lucky leaped out of the way and backed into another stack of boxes behind her. She put out her hands to catch herself to keep from falling and knocked into another stack.

As all three stacks rocked then fell, Lucky dove for the doorway, afraid she'd be crushed by bottles of liquor.

She ran into a solid wall of muscle that reached out to grab her and pull her against his chest, knocking the hat from her head. Her hair spilled out around her shoulders as the bottles crashed behind her.

"Well, look who I caught snooping around again," a male voice said.

From the room behind her, over the blare of raunchy music, she heard Audrey scream.

Jackson cursed, "Fuck! Fuck! Fuck!"

More crashing of glass sounded and Lucky stood frozen to the spot, her breath caught in her throat, praying for the floor to open up and swallow her.

When the storeroom grew quiet, she pushed hard to free herself of the hands gripping her arms, she stared up into those deep, dark, sexy brown eyes. Why did she keep running into him?

Once again he was witness to her crappy luck. She'd hoped when she left Comfort she'd leave the bad luck behind. Somehow, it had followed her all the way to the Ugly Stick Saloon.

The scent of spilled alcohol swirled around her, making her sick. "Let me go. They might be hurt."

His brows furrowed and he set her aside. "Stay," he ordered.

She stood where he set her, her heart pounding, the skin where his fingers had held her tingling.

"Audrey? You in there?" he called out.

"Yeah. Don't come in. There's broken glass everywhere."

"Where's Jackson? He came lookin' for you."

"I'm here," the man in the storeroom called out. "Fuck, the floor's so slick I can't tell what's glass and what's whiskey."

"Need me to get in there to help you out?"

"Trent, don't come in here," Audrey ordered.

Lucky couldn't stand still. She had to see how bad it was. She leaned around the man called Trent and peered into the storeroom, her empty belly clenching. "Holy hell," she whispered.

Audrey appeared from around the mound of broken containers that used to be a tall stack of boxes, pulling her shirt down over her breasts and then tugging her skirt over her hips.

The tall man with the swarthy skin of a Native American who'd helped bring the trucks out of the ditch followed her out, picking through the crushed cardboard, bottles and spilled whiskey, wine and beer.

Once she stepped out of the disaster zone, Audrey turned back to inspect the damage. "What the hell happened?"

Another town, another calamity. "It was my fault. I was the one who wrecked into your truck, and I'm the one who caused the boxes to fall." Lucky tipped her chin up. "I'll clean up the mess. I promise. And I'll pay you back, every cent," she whispered. "As soon as I can earn the money to do so."

Audrey faced Lucky, her eyes narrowed. "You did this?"

"It was an accident." Lucky held up her hands. "I didn't do it on purpose. Really."

Audrey shook her head. "Were you the one trying to get my attention?"

Lucky nodded. "I should have walked away. I tried, but I backed into the boxes while watching…uh, nothing…" Her cheeks heated and she looked at her boots. "I'm sorry."

A small, slender finger tipped her chin upward. "Hey. It's okay. No one got hurt."

Jackson glared. "Are you kidding me?"

Audrey smiled at him. "Jackson, be a dear and go check on Greta Sue." She nodded toward the other man behind Lucky. "Take Trent with you."

Trent, Mr. Tall, Dark and Sexy. Lucky's gaze followed him as he left with Jackson.

When Audrey turned back to Lucky, she gave her a gentle smile. "You can come with me." She led her into a small office with an old desk and shut the door.

"I'm so sorry." Lucky tucked her hands in her pockets to keep from wringing them. "You could have been hurt."

"But I wasn't."

"I ruined your boots," Lucky glanced at the stained red boots.

"They're things. They can be replaced." Audrey's shoulders raised and lowered. "I'll get over it."

"And the truck."

"I know a really good body guy in Hole in the Wall. He'll have it looking like new before you know it."

"I can't believe you're not ranting and raving. I would be so mad at all the stuff I've ruined."

Audrey laughed and hugged her, that one gesture was the straw that broke Lucky's control. Tears welled and she fought to keep them from sliding down her cheeks. She swiped at one that escaped. "I'm sorry. I never cry."

The other woman's eyes widened. "Why not?"

Lucky stood straighter. "My father taught me it did no good to cry. Be tough and the world won't take advantage of you."

Audrey's lips twisted and she gave Lucky a knowing grimace. "Gets old, doesn't it?"

Another tear slipped free and Lucky swiped it away, nodding. Her throat constricted with emotion. When she could finally force words past the knot she said, "I'll pay you back. Everything. The truck repairs, the bottles of alcohol. Everything." Her head tilted down. "As soon as I can earn money to do it." She glanced back up, her jaw set. "And I will."

The owner of the saloon stared at her for a long moment as if looking straight into her soul.

Lucky wanted to hide from the glance, but she stood tall and proud, despite the few tears making salty tracks down her cheeks.

"I could always use some help around here," Audrey finally said.

Her jaw fell and she blinked past the tears in her eyes. "Are you offering me work?"

Audrey nodded. "If you want it. Although it would be nice to know your name."

"Lucky Albright." She held out her hand.

The owner of the Ugly Stick Saloon gave it a firm shake with slender fingers.

Lucky debated telling her about the bad luck streak that had been following her around like a heavy black cloud for going on two years. "Are you sure?"

Audrey walked around Lucky, studying her from the top of her cowboy hat to the tips of her boots. As she circled her, the pretty owner tapped a finger to her chin. "Can you dance?"

Shaking her head, Lucky pointed at her boots. "I grew up ranchin'. I have two left feet on the dance floor. But I can ride, rope and mend a fence as good or better than any man. And I'm good with animals."

With a laugh, Audrey's eyes narrowed. "I suppose some of the cowboys can be real animals when they've had a few too many, but we don't have much call for mending fences or ropin'. Our mechanical horse is on the fritz or I'd have you ride it." Her smile returned. "Ever wait tables?"

Her hopes plummeting, Lucky shook her head. "Closest I've come to waiting tables is serving dinner to the horses, spreading hay out for the cattle, or slopping pigs."

"I can see some similarities in ranching and serving customers. It's just different drinks and food. If you're game, you can work here until you find something more your style."

Lucky stared into Audrey's eyes. "You have every right to be angry with me. To hate me and want me to leave. Why are you being so kind?"

Audrey touched her arm. "I have a sense about people. You seem nice enough and I can tell you've got a good heart. I didn't have two nickels to rub together when I came to work at the Ugly Stick Saloon. Sometimes people need a chance to start over. I know I did." She raised her hands palms up and stared around the bar. "Now I own the place." Her mouth twisted. "I wonder sometimes if that's a good thing or a bad thing. But I promised I'd help other people like the former owner helped me. Kind of paying it forward."

Lucky's heart swelled, pushing hard against her ribs. After the "good" people of Comfort had run her out of town, she'd wondered if she'd ever be accepted anywhere. And she'd accidentally stumbled on this place out in the middle of nowhere Texas. If she hadn't run out of gas, she might not have stopped. Might not have met this remarkable woman.

Lucky hugged Audrey and stepped back fast, her face burning. "I'm sorry. It's just...you know...hard to find work."

Audrey hugged her back. "I know. But you're destined for something different. You can work until you find it. And after, if you need to work extra."

"I might. I intend to pay for the repairs on your truck and for all the bottles of alcohol I broke."

"You don't have to do that."

With a shake of her head, Lucky stayed firm. "Yes, I do. When do you want me to start?"

"You can help clean up tonight." Audrey studied her. "For all your outdoor tan, you're kind of pale. When was the last time you've eaten?"

Her stomach rumbled loudly in answer. Embarrassed, Lucky glanced at her feet. "Yesterday."

"Good grief, Lucky, I'll have one of the girls whip up a burger for you."

Weak with relief, Lucky dared to think perhaps her luck had turned around. Though she was sure once she could think straight again, she'd realize it hadn't. That bad luck streak was potent and hard to kick.

"I'll go let Charli know you're a new employee and to get someone to grill up that burger." Audrey turned to leave, stopped and glanced back over her shoulder, tapping a finger to her chin. "You know, I recall seeing an ad out front for a ranch hand. I'll go look for it and let you know. In the meantime, stay put in here until I get back with that hamburger. Can't have my new waitress passing out with hunger on her first night."

"Thank you," Lucky choked out, feeling like she'd found a safe haven in the storm that had become her life over the past two years.

Left to her own devices, Lucky glanced around at the old furniture and the papers neatly stacked on the scarred, wooden desktop. Scattered around the room were photographs of Audrey and various people. Front and center was one of her and Jackson holding each other like only lovers can, the love between them apparent and so poignant it hurt for Lucky to look at them.

There were other photographs of Audrey and what looked like waitresses who worked for the Ugly Stick. They wore short shorts and cowboy boots and they all looked happy.

Maybe, just maybe, Lucky could be happy again.

Since Sean died, she hadn't had much reason to smile. If not for her, he'd still be alive today. They'd both been in the same wreck, but Sean died and she'd lived. And if it weren't for her begging to go along for the ride to Austin,

Sean wouldn't have been broadsided by an eighteen-wheeler.

You never knew when your number was going to be up. Lucky had a hard time believing it wasn't all her fault. Her luck had changed that day, and every day since had been one unlucky event or situation after another.

Fifteen minutes passed and the inactivity made Lucky antsy. With all the talk of food, the acid in her belly churned, making her feel a little nauseous. She rose and paced the interior of the office, touching photo frames and reading certificates on the walls.

Lucky had her back to the door when it opened.

Footsteps sounded behind her.

She spun to face not Audrey but a man with dark hair and dark eyes. He was as nice looking as Trent, with a more open and friendly face.

"Hi, my name's Isaac."

She took his hand and gave it a firm shake. "Lucky."

"Some say I am. And I'm beginning to think I am now that I've met you."

She laughed at his blatant flirting. "No, my name is Lucky Albright."

"That's your real name or a nickname?" Isaac asked with casual curiosity.

"My mother must have been feeling lucky that day. It's on my birth certificate that way."

"Well, then I'll definitely consider this as my *lucky* day." Isaac grinned. "Nice to meet you, Lucky. Audrey tells me you're looking for a job on a ranch."

"I am."

"I have a ranch."

"That's nice."

"And I'm in need of a ranch hand."

"You are?" Her pulse hammered. Maybe her luck really had changed. "I'm available during the day." She nodded toward the door. "Audrey offered me a job waiting tables at night. I need to pay her back for wrecking her truck and storeroom."

"You wrecked her storeroom too?" Isaac's grin widened. "That's some lousy luck."

Lucky held her breath, waiting for Isaac to pass on offering her a job.

Instead, he clapped his hands together. "So, what kind of ranch experience have you had?"

Lucky told him all she'd done working on the ranch where her father had been foreman—deeding animals, castrating steers, exercising thoroughbred and quarter horses. "I'm an excellent rider. I'm familiar with various riding styles that include English and western, reining and racing. I prefer western-style riding. I know how to use a come-along to stretch fence and I think I've built and repaired enough fencing to surround this county. I can also drive most tractors. I've cut, baled and hauled hay, cleared fields, planted and harvested crops and most of all, I'm good with all ranch animals." She stopped to take a breath and gauge Isaac's response.

"I believe I've found the perfect woman." He pressed his hand to his chest and then held it out. "You're hired."

Lucky gripped his hand and could almost feel the weight lift from her shoulders. "I am?"

"If you can do all that stuff, you're just what we need."

"We?"

"My partner and I can't do it all ourselves. An extra pair of hands will go a long way to helping out. Especially someone who knows his—er—her way around animals and hard work. When can you start?"

"Immediately." She laughed. "At least bright and early in the morning."

"You're new to town, right?"

"I am."

"Have you found a place to stay?"

"No."

"Then you can stay at the ranch house."

She grinned. Two jobs and a place to live. How much better could life get? Her happiness faded. "Only one thing."

"What's that?"

Her face burned. "I'll need a ride out to the ranch." She hurried to add, "Just until I can earn enough to put gas in my truck."

Isaac pulled his wallet out of his back pocket and removed a couple of twenties. "Get that gas. Can't have my new employee hitching rides."

"I can't accept what I haven't earned."

"Sweetheart, you'll earn it. I promise you." He gave her directions to the Triple J Ranch, tipped his cowboy hat and smiled. "You can have the guest bedroom."

Clutching the bills in her fist, she threw her arms around his neck and kissed him on the cheek. "Thank you so very much."

His smile widening, he set her away from him. "Can't say I've ever been kissed by a ranch hand. You're my first." He rubbed his cheek. "I kinda liked it. Well, I better be going. My partner will be waiting impatiently. Speaking of which, expect a little resistance. Most likely he'll be expecting a ranch hand of the opposite gender."

"I'll show him I can do anything a man can do, only better."

"I'm sure you will, and more." He left, chuckling.

Forty bucks in her hand, two jobs to get her by and a place to lay her head. Yup, her luck was changing.

Lucky was still grinning when Audrey returned with a Styrofoam tray filled with a fat, juicy hamburger, dripping with grease and a pile of fries enough for four people.

"Eat up and get your strength. That storeroom will likely take a couple hours to clean." Audrey patted her shoulder. "Don't worry. You won't have to do it all by yourself."

"Oh, but I want to. Since I made the mess, I expect to clean it. Plus it'll give me chance to inventory the damages, so I'll know what I owe you." Although she owed her more than the damages.

Audrey had given her a second chance. She intended to make good on that opportunity.

Now if only her luck would hold.

CHAPTER FOUR

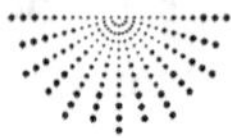

Isaac sat in a rocking chair on the front porch of the ranch house, waiting for Lucky to arrive, hoping she wouldn't until Trent was fast asleep in his bed with the overhead fan drowning out all the softer noises. He hadn't told his brother he'd hired a woman ranch hand and he didn't plan on telling him any sooner than he had to. He relished the look on his face when he discovered her gender.

And from what Lucky had told him, she'd be just as good if not better than any male ranch hand that didn't have nearly the amount of experience she claimed to have.

If she didn't work out, well, no harm, no foul. He'd let her go. She had her job at the Ugly Stick to fall back on. He'd liked her on the spot and really hoped this little experiment worked out.

Trent poked his head through the door and asked, "Aren't you going to hit the rack?"

"In a bit. I'm enjoying the night air, peace and quiet after the noise of the Ugly Stick."

Trent stepped out on the porch, walked to the edge and leaned against one of the support beams.

"You have to admit this is one of the only places you've ever been where you can hear yourself think," Isaac said softly. He'd tried to bring Trent over to his way of thinking. He knew how hard their father had been on him and that he'd treated him badly, always demanding more than he had to give and punishing him harshly when he didn't live up to John Jameson's expectations. Which was practically always.

The times Isaac had stepped in and disagreed with his father, he'd gotten the same treatment and Trent got twice the severity. He'd learned early on to stay out of it. It saved Trent additional grief.

He understood why Trent hated the ranch, but he wanted Trent to see that it wasn't the place that was bad, but their father's mistreatment. The Triple J Ranch was perfect now that John Jameson no long ran roughshod over his sons. The old man was probably rolling over in his grave at how they were running the operation since he'd been gone, but Isaac didn't care.

They needed help but hadn't pursued it yet, probably more out of cussed determination to prove to their dead father they could get along just fine without him.

Up until Dusty had knee replacement, they had managed fine. Granted it took a lot of their free time and their regular jobs had suffered for it, but they'd proven, if not to their dead father then to themselves, that they could manage the ranch.

Now they needed help.

"It is peaceful here." Trent's comment was low, almost lost in the faint breeze.

"It's ours now. We can do whatever we want with it."

"Like sell?"

Isaac didn't comment. He'd said all he was going to say, even telling Trent he refused to sell. If his brother still felt the same in a year, he would relent. But he had to at least give it a year. If Trent couldn't let go of the old hurt and anger a year after their father's death, he never would and it would be time to let go of a place that only held bad memories.

"Do you really like living in Houston?"

"It's closer to my work."

"You can design structures from anywhere and get your work delivered on time. It's the beauty of satellite Internet and express shipping. And I go when and where I need to."

"As long as we have an able-bodied foreman to leave the ranch with. Which we don't have."

"He'll be back." Isaac wasn't ready to break the news to Trent about the new hire. Not right before Trent would hopefully go to bed.

"Not soon enough."

"Getting itchy feet?" Isaac asked.

Trent hesitated. "I don't have the connection to this place you seem to have."

"Have you given it a fair shake?" Isaac stood. "I mean, really given it a chance since Dad died?"

Trent continued to stare out at the Texas landscape bathed in indigo-blue moonlight. "I'm going to bed. There's a fence down on the northeast corner. I want to get out there early and get it up before the cattle discover it and wander off."

"I'm right behind you in a little bit. I'm still unwinding from the fun at the Ugly Stick. We should play poker every Ladies Night."

"I'm surprised you didn't bring one of the ladies home. Or better yet, go home with one."

Isaac hid a grin in the dark. "I can be picky too."

Trent snorted. "You've dated just about every woman in the tri-county area and you've yet to settle down. I'm not the only one who doesn't like to commit."

"I know. I have to admit, I'm just as picky when considering a lifelong promise to love, honor and cherish."

"You could always go for Kylie Sandell." Trent left that jab hanging.

"Not in a million years. She and her mother are toxic."

"Speaking of toxic, we promised a load of fertilizer to be delivered to Mrs. Sandell's house. She asked for horse dung for her rose garden."

"Only the best for her prize roses." Isaac's eyes narrowed. "Why did you promise to deliver it to her? You know she'll pick it apart."

"She's an older woman. I was taught to respect my elders, especially women."

"You could have said no."

"I know, but it's done. I made a promise and I'll deliver on that promise."

Isaac sighed. "I'll help. Someone needs to watch your back. That Kylie is as sly and conniving as her mother. The rotten apple didn't fall far from the poison apple tree."

Trent chuckled. "Good night."

"Good night." Isaac breathed a sigh of relief when Trent finally went inside.

He listened for the sounds of his brother entering and exiting the bathroom and finally the house fell silent.

Checking his watch, he noted it was thirty minutes past midnight. The Ugly Stick closed at midnight on Thursdays, even when it was Ladies Night. Before he'd left the saloon, he'd askedAudrey if he could use the five-gallon jug of gasoline she kept on hand for the bar's lawn-care equipment. Thankfully, she'd filled it the day before. He'd poured all five gallons into Lucky's truck. That should have been enough to get her to the truck stop in Temptation where she could use the forty dollars he'd given her to fill her tank. If all went well and she didn't have trouble following his directions, she'd be driving up the driveway in the next five minutes.

Headlights shined through the trees heading up the road to the ranch.

Isaac stepped off the porch and waved Lucky to park on the side of the house Trent rarely visited, hoping the lights wouldn't alert Trent to a visitor at this late hour.

When Lucky turned off her lights and climbed down from the old pickup, she smiled. "You didn't have to stay up and wait for me to come. But thanks."

"I didn't want you tripping in the dark, trying to find your way around." Isaac turned toward the house. "If you'll follow me."

When he didn't hear her behind him, he turned to see her standing with her back to him, staring up at the night sky. "Wow. I didn't know how much I missed this."

"Missed what?"

"The night sky."

"Have you been living in a city?"

"Not a city, but I've been living in a small town outside of San Antonio. Even the small towns have a lot of lights that shine all night."

"I can wait to show you to your room if you want to sit out on the porch for a while."

"Do you mind?" She gave him a tentative smile. "After the noise of the saloon, this is heaven."

"Sure. Let me get your gear, then you can come sit on the steps with me."

"The boxes can stay in the backseat. I just need my clothes." She grabbed a duffel bag from behind the seat and slung the strap over her shoulder.

"I'll get that." Isaac took the bag from her.

"I'm a ranch hand. I don't expect special treatment just because I'm a girl."

"I know, but chivalry isn't dead." He slung the bag over his shoulder. "Humor me."

"You're the boss." She followed him to the porch, dropped the duffel bag and sat down on the steps, leaning back on her elbows. "It's beautiful."

Isaac sat beside her and leaned back on his elbows as well. "*I* think so."

"Someone else doesn't?"

"My partner thinks he wants to move back to Houston."

Lucky shot a glance at Isaac. "I personally can't see how anyone would prefer Houston over this."

"Me either." Isaac continued to stare at the night sky. "Tell me about yourself, Lucky."

She stiffened beside him. "You might not want me to work for you if I tell you about myself."

Isaac chuckled. "Unless you're a convicted felon, I can't imagine you've done anything fire-worthy."

Lucky hesitated. "Well, actually…"

"I won't believe if it if you tell me you've killed someone, unless it was justifiable homicide."

She laughed and relaxed a little. "No, I haven't killed anyone that I know, but you might as well know now." With a deep breath, she told him, "I have an unlucky streak the size of Texas."

Isaac wiped his hand across his forehead. "Whew! For a

minute there I thought it was something big."

"Maybe you don't understand." Lucky faced him. "The good people of Comfort, Texas, ran me out of town because of my bad luck."

He laughed and stopped mid-chuckle at the serious look on her face. Lucky really believed her luck was the issue.

"I mean look at what's happened already. I pushed Audrey's truck into a ditch and destroyed half her liquor stores. I'm bad luck." Though tears welled in her eyes, she didn't let one loose. She bit into her lip, making Isaac want to pull her close and kiss her troubles away.

"Ah, Lucky. It can't be that bad." He couldn't resist and gathered her in his arms.

"Since my father died, I have no home to go to. But the real bad luck started the day my fiancé was killed in a car wreck. A wreck I should have died in too."

Isaac's chest tightened. "Oh, baby, I'm sorry you lost your fiancé, but I'm glad you didn't die in that wreck."

She leaned into him, her cheek resting against his shoulder. "I'm not looking for sympathy. I'm just tired." She looked to the stars. "Tired of things going wrong around me, tired of moving on." With a soft snort, she gave him a crooked smile. "Most people don't know how lucky they have it."

The faraway look in her face and the hollow tone in her voice nailed it for Isaac. He held her, his arms secure around her. "You must have loved him a lot."

"I did, but it's been two years. I'm finally getting over it, but my luck hasn't changed. I really wish it would."

"You've had some tough breaks."

"I didn't come here to cry over my crappy life," she said into his shirt, without pulling away. "But thanks."

After a while, he pushed her to arm's length. "Did you ever consider that maybe your streak of bad luck brought you here? To Temptation, the Ugly Stick Saloon and the Triple J Ranch? Do you believe in fate?"

She leaned back, looked at him and shrugged. "Mostly when she slaps me in the face."

"I believe fate brought you here and you're just what the Triple J Ranch needed. And maybe the Triple J is what you need to get back on track."

"I hope so."

"Here's to starting over." He waved his hand in the air.

"Please tell me you sprinkled some magic dust with that wave."

"Better. Consider your slate wiped clean. Lucky Albright has only good things ahead of her."

Lucky didn't look as confident as he felt. Isaac leaned forward and brushed her lips with his, liking the feel of hers. All soft and plump. Ripe for kissing.

Lucky's eyes widened and her lips opened on a gasp. "What was that for?"

"For good luck." He pulled her against him and kissed her again, this time lingering over the connection, his tongue darting out to skim the seam of her mouth.

"And that?" she whispered.

"That was because I couldn't resist a beautiful woman in the moonlight." He smiled down at her and pulled her to her feet.

She leaned up on her toes and kissed him back.

He laughed. "And what was that for?"

"I like the way you taste."

"I could get used to you around here."

The sad look in her eyes faded and she smiled.

Isaac's heart flipped. Hell, the moonlight had nothing

on Lucky's smile. Her face lit up half the county and made him want to laugh out loud with joy. He could spend a lifetime making her smile. "You have a beautiful smile."

Her smile faded to just a hint of one and she glanced down at her feet. "Thank you."

With a finger beneath her chin, he tipped her head up. When she stared up into his face, his entire body lit on fire. The woman had no clue how desirable she was. For a moment, he hesitated, considering crushing her to his chest and taking more than a chaste kiss. But then he was afraid of scaring her on her first night at the ranch. Drawing in a deep breath, he let it out, willing his pulse to stop banging so hard. "It's getting late. Let me show you to your room."

"I am tired."

"Right. Look, Lucky, I haven't told my partner about you yet. I thought I'd give you a chance to show him what you're made of before I break it to him that I've hired a ranch hand."

Lucky pulled free of his hand. "You haven't told him?"

"No."

"And he won't like it that you've hired a woman. Most cowboys wouldn't." It was a statement, not a question.

Isaac winked. "You got it. Thus the need to show him you can handle the work before he has a chance to say no."

"Does he make all the decisions?"

"No, but it helps to get his buy-in. He can be cranky when he wants to be." Isaac stood, pulled her to her feet and snagged her duffel bag.

"I'll consider myself warned." Lucky followed Isaac up the stairs. "And don't worry. I'm a very good ranch hand."

"I'm counting on it." Isaac slipped an arm around her waist and ushered her into the house. "And you're much better looking than any of the other hands on any ranch I've ever been to."

Isaac had to admit to himself he'd hired Lucky on a lark, partly because they needed a ranch hand, but mostly because he knew the fact she was female would get under his brother's skin.

But now that he knew she was honest enough to own up to the baggage that came with her, he liked her even more. What a bunch of horseshit the last town she'd lived in had heaped onto her. No one deserved to be kicked out of town for a bad streak of luck.

Lucky seemed genuine, just the type of girl Isaac had searched for all his life and that even Trent had said he was looking for. No pretense, no frills, pretty without being conscious of the fact, and a good hard worker.

Yeah, his and Trent's luck was about to change and he looked forward to having Lucky around making it happen. And if he could steal another kiss from her and maybe more, well, that was just icing on the cake.

Lucky followed Isaac to the last bedroom at the end of the hallway, her mind on the kiss and the way Isaac made her feel when he held her in his arms—safe and warm, and burning hot at the same time. The cowboy from earlier that evening had left her feeling hot, twitchy and off balance, and yet she'd craved kisses from both men. And if she was honest with herself, a whole lot more. It had been a long time since she'd made love to a man.

When Isaac pushed the door open, he left the light off. Moonlight poured through the window, filling the room with a deep blue glow. Her gaze went straight for the bed and her blood pulsed, driving heat to her belly and lower.

He applied a slight pressure to the small of her back, ushering her through the doorway. "If you need anything, my room is right across the hall." He turned her, his hand sliding around to her hip. "And I mean anything."

"Even a kiss?" she said, before she could think about what she was starting.

He smiled. "That goes without saying." He bent, his mouth coming down over hers, his lips claiming hers in a sensuous stroke.

She leaned up on her toes, her fingers circling the back of his neck, urging him closer. Lucky parted her lips, allowing his tongue inside to glide along hers. He tasted of mint.

He cupped her bottom and lifted her, wrapping her legs around him, pressing her breasts against his chest. "Stop me if I'm going too fast."

For a moment she considered it, but after the craziness of the day, she needed to feel wanted, and wanted to feel needed. "What if your partner wakes?"

"Let him get his own woman."

"Isaac." Lucky braced her hands on either side of his face. "Just for the record, I'm not your woman."

He grinned. "I'm sorry. You're right and I know that." His grin faded. "So what is this?"

"Two people taking advantage of moonlight?"

"Works for me." He kicked the door shut behind them. "And maybe when we get to know each other better, I'll convince you otherwise."

He laid her in the middle of the bed and pushed her tank top up, trailing kisses along her belly.

Lucky writhed against the sheets. "Wow, that feels nice."

"You think so?" He pushed the shirt up higher,

exposing her lacy bra. She thanked the heavens for the miracle of dirty laundry. Normally she wore simple cotton bras because they didn't itch as much when she worked out in the heat. Feeling feminine and sexy, she allowed him to pull the shirt up over her head and toss it to the floor.

He reached around her back and flipped the hooks open, sliding the straps down her arms, her breasts spilling out.

Lucky had always been a little self-conscious about her breasts. Growing up as a tomboy, they were annoying and in the way. Not until she'd met Sean had she realized how prized they were by men.

Isaac cupped one with his big, rough hand and flicked the nipple with the tip of his tongue.

"Sweet tea and grits!" she called out.

He chuckled and did it again.

Her back arched off the bed as if it had a mind of its own, pushing her breast deeper into Isaac's mouth. Lucky's breath caught and held, waiting for him to stroke her again.

When he did, a sharp zing of electricity sang through her veins, headed south to her core, awakening fires long banked. She feverishly worked the buttons on his chambray shirt, desire pushing her faster. Nothing less than skin on skin would do. When she released the last button, she pushed the shirt over his shoulders.

He leaned back, shucked the shirt and stood and slipped out of his jeans.

Lucky's throat dried and her tongue swiped over her lips.

The man was beautiful, not an ounce of fat anywhere. His shoulders were wide, his arms bulged with well-defined muscles and his broad chest narrowed to a trim waist.

As her gaze wandered farther south, her belly tightened and her eyes widened. His cock jutted out long, hard and thick. Her pussy clenched, a wash of juices slicking the channel in anticipation.

When he reached for the snap on her jeans, she suddenly became conscious of where she was and what she was doing. "Wait." She crossed her hands over her crotch. "We really shouldn't. You're the boss. I didn't come to the Triple J to seduce you."

Isaac laughed aloud. "You're seducing me?"

She frowned. "Well, yes."

"Then I'm not doing this right." He shook his head, urging her hands aside with his. Then he bent to kiss her along the waistband of her jeans. "I should be wooing you, making you crazy with desire until you lose yourself in the moment." He blew a stream of warm air into the gap between her jeans and her belly, then kissed her skin there. "I should make you want me so much that you wouldn't even realize I was stripping the clothes from your beauti-ful, incredibly sexy body."

"I'm not beautiful," she said, but she didn't stop him when he tugged the zipper down and dragged her jeans from her legs.

His gazed raked over her from her breasts to her sex, his eyes darkening in the moonlight. "You don't see what I see."

"No, but I see you." Caught up in his seduction, she reached out to touch his hip, her hand sliding over the hard contours of his ass, loving how taut and firm he was.

His fingers wove through the hair at the apex of her thighs, parting her folds to that little nubbin she'd been stroking when she'd watched Audrey and Jackson get it on in the storeroom. The image of the lovers going at it among the boxes sent blasts of lust through her, and she let her knees fall to the side, inviting him in.

His first stroke against her clit had her digging her heels into the mattress. The second made her rise to greet the third and fourth. "If this is seduction, I'm a complete amateur."

Isaac parted her folds and bent, placing his face close to her pulsing clit and blowing on the hot little bundle of excited nerves.

Her eyes widened and she tensed. "What are you doing?"

"I'm sealing the deal. Once you've had this, there will be no going back."

Unable to move, she watched in total fascination as his tongue slipped out and tapped the strip of flesh.

Nerve endings erupted in an explosion of sensations, centering at her core and shooting outward to her entire body tingling with awareness.

"Sweet tea and grits!" she cried again.

Isaac laughed. "What did you say?"

"Oh, please. Don't stop now."

With a reassuring smile, he complied, sending her up and over the edge, her body rocking into an earth-shattering orgasm. When she thought she couldn't take any more, he quit, pulled his wallet from his back jeans pocket and dug a condom out of its folds.

Still writhing from the extreme pleasure of his tongue, Lucky couldn't wait and welcomed him when he thrust into her drenched channel.

He filled her, stretching her, sliding deep inside.

"Okay?" He held still for a moment.

"More than okay," she replied, shocked by the breathlessness of her voice.

He continued in slow, steady moves, building in speed and strength.

Lucky returned to ecstasy with him until, once again, she cried out, her body tightening, her breathing ragged, catching with the intensity.

Isaac thrust once more and held steady, his jaw tight, his eyes closed, his cock throbbing against her channel.

When at last Isaac collapsed on the bed beside her, Lucky lay against the bed, her thoughts spinning as she returned to earth and reality. She had just made love with one of her new bosses.

Damn. Had she screwed things up yet again?

Isaac lay on the bed beside her, brushing his hand along her arm. "Whatcha thinking?"

"I'm thinking you should leave and let me get some sleep."

His hand stilled and he withdrew it. "Okay. I know this is all new to you. I'll give you your space. But this can't be over. That was too damned incredible." He rolled out of the bed and stood beside her, naked and too handsome for her to look away.

"It might have to be. I should never have done that." She pulled the sheet up over her naked body. "I'm here to prove myself as a ranch hand."

"And I vow to prove that you can and will be much more than that." He lifted her hand and kissed her knuckles. "Good night, Lucky. Sweet dreams."

TRENT WOKE IN A GROUCHY MOOD. Hell, he hadn't slept much and when he did he dreamed about her. The tall, slender cowgirl who'd captured his attention at the Ugly Stick Saloon last night. He found himself still wanting that kiss she'd refused to give him.

Telling himself it was *because* she'd refused him that he still wanted it. He always wanted what he couldn't have and took it as a challenge to acquire it.

But he had to know more about the woman than just what she looked like. A name would have been a start. Her phone number would be even better. He had neither and he'd woken up with a hard-on thinking about her, which added to his bad mood and frustration.

Dressing quickly, he pulled on his boots and passed through the house, entering the kitchen with no intention of eating. In his mood, he'd do everyone a favor by working off his frustration before he tried making conversation.

"Hey, the ad paid off. I hired someone." Isaac sat at the table, a plate of scattered crumbs in front of him, a coffee mug in one hand, the newspaper in the other.

Trent stopped long enough to glare at his brother. "That quickly? How come I didn't get to interview this ranch hand?"

Isaac glanced up from the newspaper. "It's a done deal. If it doesn't work out, we can hire someone else. In the meantime we have help."

"When does he start?"

Isaac opened his mouth to reply, hesitated, then said, "Today."

Trent snorted. "Good. We could use the help. I hope he's good."

"I'm sure you'll be surprised at how good." Isaac ducked behind the newspaper, a smirk on his face.

Trent's eyes narrowed, but he'd already reached

conversation saturation point for the morning and he was still grumpy and frustrated.

Though he could use a cup of coffee, he didn't want to be bothered with more talk, so he pushed through the back screen door and strode across the yard.

The day before, he and Isaac had hauled hay and stacked it inside the barn. They'd been hot and tired when they'd stacked it and it wasn't exactly as good as it could be in Trent's opinion. Which was just fine with him. Hell, rearranging the bales ought to work the kinks out of his mood.

Trent went to work stacking the hay on another wall, one bale at a time. Halfway through the stack, his muscles burned and he'd worked up a good sweat. He was feeling better and had almost forgotten the woman at the saloon.

With several tall columns of bales leaning against one wall, Trent was about to start a stack in front of them when a noise made him turn around.

A slim figure in jeans and a chambray shirt entered Thunder's horse stall.

Thunder hadn't been ridden since Dusty the ranch foreman had been tossed and ended up in the hospital.

Trent started to say something to the new ranch hand about the horse and his temperament. Before he could, the hand emerged, leading a placid Thunder out by his lead rope. If the horse had an attitude, it wasn't on display that morning.

The cowboy had his head dipped, his cowboy hat pulled low. Between the dim lighting in the barn and the shadows from the rim of his hat, Trent couldn't see the cowboy's face. Covered in sweat and hay, Trent didn't feel much like introducing himself yet. But he watched as the young man led the horse out of the barn. A few minutes later, he returned and entered the stall with the wheelbarrow, and soon had a pile of soiled straw loaded into it.

Trent resumed his work on the hay, keeping a watch on the new guy from the corner of his eye.

One stall after the other the young cowboy worked. When he completed the last stall and was pushing the last wheelbarrow load of soiled straw toward the door, Trent decided it was time to inspect the job and introduce himself.

"Wait up, there." Trent tossed the bale he'd been carrying, dusted the straw off his gloves and crossed to the ranch hand. He glanced past the man's shoulder into the cleaned stall and noted it was cleaner than he or Isaac usually got it. "Name's Trent Jameson." He held out his hand. "Nice work you've been doin' there."

For a moment the cowboy froze. Then gripped Trent's hand with his own gloved one. "Thanks." The cowboy refused to look up, keeping his chin tucked in, his head lowered.

Trent couldn't look the man in the eye. He didn't trust a man who wouldn't look him directly in the eye. "You got a name?"

"Lucky."

"Lucky." Trent digested that. "Nickname?"

The ranch hand shook his head and tipped his hat lower over his head. "I better go dump this." As he hurried around Trent, the wheel ran over Trent's toe.

"Ow!" Trent yanked his foot back and teetered on one leg.

"Oh my gosh!" The cowboy's hands flew in the air and the wheelbarrow dumped over, the contents rushing out, knocking Trent backward. He slammed into the freshly stacked hay bales and they swayed.

Trent glanced up, his breath hitching.

Crap.

"Oh no." The young cowboy launched himself at the hay, tripped over the pile of dung and straw and, instead of catching the bales before they toppled, sprawled out on top of Trent.

The bales tipped and fell, one after the other, landing on or near them.

Several grunts sounded from the cowboy who took the bulk of the pummeling.

His hat flew off and long sandy-blonde hair tangled with the loose hay flying around the interior of the barn.

Trent blinked the hay and dust out of his eyes and stared up into pretty gray eyes, the color of storm clouds. "You!"

The woman he'd been dreaming about kissing planted her hands against his chest and tried to push herself off him.

"Yes, me."

He opened his mouth to admit he thought he'd never see her again. Thinking better of it, he demanded, "What the hell are you doing here?"

"Working." Jerking her leg out from under a heavy bale, she managed to roll off him and onto the ground. "What does it look like?" As agile as a cat, she shot to her feet.

"I can see that. But why?"

"Isaac hired me as the new ranch hand."

"What?" Trent stood and stared at her.

"Is it so hard to believe a woman can be as effective and efficient at ranch work as a man?"

"I didn't say that."

"No, you didn't have to." She stood, brushing the hay from her jeans but missing the straws stuck in her hair.

"Now, if you'll excuse me, I'm going to get to work cleaning this up."

"I didn't say I agreed with Isaac's decision to hire you."

She planted her hands on her hips. "You gonna fire me?"

He glared at her. "I don't know."

"Well, until you say otherwise, I have work to do."

Trent climbed over the bales to stand in front of her. "Like I said last night. You're trouble."

Something clouded her already stormy eyes. "Maybe, but I work hard and I know my way around a ranch."

She grabbed a bale and threw it up onto the stack.

"I gathered that." And she was beautiful with fire in her eyes and hay in her hair. Trent worked alongside her until they had all the hay stacked in neat rows. When they were done, he brushed straw off his body and grinned. She'd worked hefting as many bales as he had. So, she could lift bales.

Lucky flicked hay off her shoulders. "If we're done here, there's a fence on the northeast corner of the property I intend to fix."

"You can't do that."

"Why not?" she asked.

"Because it's a two-man—person—job."

"I've strung fence with and without help. I can handle it."

"Maybe so, but we use the buddy rule around here. Unless you're working around the house or barn, you always take a buddy with you. That way if one or the other is hurt, you have someone there to help."

She looked at him through slitted eyes. "You're making that up."

He held up two fingers. "Scout's honor."

Her eyes narrowed even more. "When were you ever a Scout?"

His lips twisted. "Okay, so I've never been a Scout. But we do use the buddy system. I'll go with you."

Her full, soft lips tightened. "How do you usually get there?"

"I take the four-wheeler. You can ride on the back."

"Is that how you and your partner…er, brother ride out?"

"We usually take a couple of four-wheelers, but one of them is in the shop for repair."

She hesitated then nodded. "Okay. Let's go."

Trent gathered the come-along, a roll of barbed wire, pliers, a hammer and a couple of metal fence posts and the heavy pounder used to drive them in.

Lucky took half of the supplies and carried them out into the open, then went back for the other half while Trent pulled the four-wheeler out of one of the storage areas in the barn.

Loading what she could in the box on the back, she settled the fence posts over the box and Trent strapped them down along with the pole pounder.

"I'll get my hat and be ready to go." Lucky disappeared into the barn.

Isaac joined Trent, carrying two water bottles. He settled them in the box with the tools. "I take it you've met our new ranch hand."

Trent gave Isaac a withering look. "Yeah. You could have warned me."

"She has the experience and know-how. And from the looks of it, the stamina." Isaac's lips twitched.

"Don't go there."

"Well, she's a lot easier on the eye than some of the

ranch hands I've seen hanging out at the Ugly Stick."

"We needed someone to do the job, not someone to stare at. Dusty's not coming back for another two months." He'd done his share of staring and Isaac was right. The woman was a looker. Not a traditional beauty, more statuesque and fresh-faced all at once. She didn't wear makeup or hairspray in her hair, but she had a natural beauty and her skin glowed with good health.

"So if she doesn't work out, we hire someone else and let her go." Isaac's face brightened. "Hey, maybe she can cook."

"What's wrong with my cookin'?" Trent asked.

Isaac snorted. "Nothing if you like everything burned to charcoal."

"I don't burn everything."

"All you ever do is grill."

Trent's brows rose in challenge. "And you're any better?"

"No. That's my point."

"Just because she's female doesn't mean she can cook."

"True. But I like her. A lot." Isaac turned a big smile at Lucky as she emerged from the barn. "Ah, there you are. Something you should know. The newest ranch hand on the ranch has K.P. duty for the first week."

Her brows furrowed. "K.P.?"

"Kitchen patrol. You're cookin' tonight."

"But I—"

Isaac's shoulders rose and lowered. "It's one of the rules of livin' at the Triple J Ranch." He raised his fingers like a Scout. "I swear."

Lucky cocked her head toward Trent. "He's never been a Scout either, right?"

Trent's mouth quivered as he fought laughter. "Right."

"Fine. But be warned. I'm not much good in the kitchen." She glanced at Trent. "You ready?"

"I am." He mounted the four-wheeler and Lucky slipped onto the back, her hands resting lightly on his waist.

Isaac frowned. "Hey, where are you two going?"

"From what I hear, there's a fence needing fixin' on the northeast corner. See ya this afternoon." Trent goosed the throttle and the four-wheeler took off with a jerk, forcing Lucky to wrap her arms around his middle. That was one way to get the woman to hold him.

Ranching suddenly had a new appeal to Trent, one he'd never known existed. If Lucky didn't work out as a ranch hand, he might still get that kiss he'd been hankerin' after. Then he'd have her out of his system and he could get back to his regular, grumpy, frustrated self.

LUCKY HELD on as they bumped across pastures. She got off at each gate, opening and closing them behind the ATV. Each time, Trent took off with a jerk and she had to hold on tighter or risk being left on her ass in the grass.

Riding on the back of the four-wheeler gave her the needed time to digest her feelings and pull herself together.

Had she known Isaac and Trent were co-owners of the Triple J Ranch…

What?

She sure as hell wouldn't have done the nasty with Isaac. But would she have given up the chance to work there? Declining a real job offer so that she could go pound the pavement to find something that suited her as well?

Not hardly. And she was only working nights at the

Ugly Stick Saloon. Based on her first visit there, she might be more of a disaster working there and be fired before the first full night.

The previous night she'd spent cleaning up the storeroom mess. She didn't count any of that time as paid hours she could use toward reducing her debt to Audrey. But now that she had an idea of how much she'd destroyed due to her carelessness, she could start paying off that part of what she owed Audrey.

Lucky couldn't get over how warm and friendly Audrey had been when she had all but ruined her business and truck.

She'd vowed to make it right and she would.

In the meantime, if she wanted to keep the job on the Triple J Ranch she'd likely have to work twice as hard as any man just to prove she was good at the job.

So be it.

Working at the Ugly Stick, she could put feelers out to other ranchers. If things didn't work out at the Triple J, she'd consider moving on and have a plan in place to ease her transition.

Though things had started out shaky, after looking at it from all angles, it was not one of her worst disasters. She'd make it through this one easily.

Her challenge would be resisting her bosses.

Isaac had been nothing but nice, chivalrous and so damned sexy when he'd kissed her the night before, she hadn't been able to resist. She could see herself falling for his charm and cheerful demeanor and he'd been so good in bed, gentle, caring, everything a lover should be. Her heart raced at the image of a naked Isaac pulling her into his arms. Yes, she could fall for the nicer brother.

Trent Jameson was the one who had her worried. Not only

had he tried to blackmail her for a kiss, he was entirely too attractive in that bad-boy way for a mere mortal woman to resist. Even a woman who fancied herself a cowboy. Yes, she'd been a tomboy since she knew the difference between men and women. But she was also a woman with needs and the hormones to remind her of those needs. She'd denied herself for way too long and now her needs were clouding her brain.

Riding with her legs wrapped around Trent, her breasts pressed against his back, her pulse was pounding, and she was in a lather. And for the second time in two years her girlie parts were hot, wet and ready for more than mending fences could satisfy.

She hopped off the ATV and put some distance between her and the man causing her the disconcerting feelings. Hell, she'd already been with his brother. It would be wrong to have these lusty feelings for Trent.

The bad boy tilted his head to the side. "The fence is over here."

"I know. I was just stretching the kinks out of my legs." And trying to rein in her raging desire that had other places aching to be touched.

Trent adjusted his jeans and untied the fence posts and pole pounder from the top of the utility box on the back of the ATV.

By the time he'd thrown them on the ground, Lucky was back in control. Or so she told herself.

She reached for the hammer, nails and barbed wire, her hand colliding with his, sending shock waves up her arm and back to her core, making it ache even more.

Maybe she should just give him that kiss he'd wanted the night before. She could hope he was a terrible kisser and she'd be over him before anything started.

She glanced at him. Those full lips curled upward on the ends like he knew a secret. The secret that she was as horny as the women at Ladies Night out the previous night. The night before with his brother had only stirred in her a desire for more.

Fire burned up her neck into her cheeks. She spun away and went to work, praying they'd finish quickly and she could go back to the barn. Surely there would be more horseshit to muck. Backbreaking, disgusting work would wipe this man's sexy presence out of her mind.

She'd made it all the way to the broken fence without the wire cutters before she got her head back on straight. Turning back to the ATV, her breath caught and lodged in her throat.

Trent had chosen that moment to remove his shirt and hang it on one of the posts and then bent to check the loose strands.

All the air left Lucky's lungs in a rush and for a moment she felt light-headed.

The man could make a helluva living stripping. She'd pay top dollar. And she could forget about forgetting him. No amount of horse droppings or sweaty labor would put that image out of her mind.

Her knees shaking for the second time in as many days, she snapped her gaping mouth shut, grabbed for the wire cutters and hurried back to the fence.

Using the wire cutters, she clipped the broken barbed wire.

It had just enough tension left in it to spring back.

"Fuck!" Trent yelled.

As soon as the curse word left his mouth, Lucky knew what she'd done wrong. She'd been in such a hurry to get to work, she'd forgotten how barbed wire could curl up again when the tension was released.

Cringing, she turned toward Trent and gasped.

The strand of barbed wire had wrapped around his bare chest, digging into his skin, each barb poking a hole. Blood dripped in many places.

"Sweet tea and grits!" She hurried toward him.

"Don't touch," he said, his voice curt, his mouth set in a grim line.

"But I have to get you out of that." She searched for the ends of the wire.

"You can't unwind it." He hissed, easing one of the barbs away from his skin. "You have to cut away each barb."

With the wire cutters still in her hand, she moved close to him, carefully stepping over the wire on the ground.

"I'm so sorry. I should have remembered."

"Just get it off before I bleed to death."

Slowly and with as gentle a touch as possible, she cut on each side of the barbs until those digging into him were removed and he could step free of the rest of the wire.

"Good thing each four-wheeler is equipped with a first-aid kit," he muttered. "You can find it in the utility box."

Lucky pointed to the ATV. "Sit there while I take care of the wounds."

He flexed his arms. "It's not that bad now that I'm not a human pincushion."

"Please. I feel bad enough. At least let me clean them and put antibiotic ointment on them."

"On one condition." His mouth curved upward.

"A kiss?" She sighed. "If that's what will make you sit…fine."

He settled on the seat and waited.

Lucky hovered close by, alcohol pads and a tube of

ointment in her hand. "Now? Aren't you in pain?"

"More than you know." His fingers closed around her wrist and he dragged her close. "I promise to be a very good patient."

"You'd better be." She frowned, knowing a kiss would be a very bad idea. With a quick peck on the cheek her plan, she leaned toward him, aiming for one of those high cheekbones, though the jaw line covered in rough-looking stubble called to her as well.

He must have guessed her intent and thwarted it by turning his head at the last minute, putting his lips square in line with hers. Before she could squeak a protest, he wrapped his hand around the back of her head and crushed her lips with his.

To keep from falling into him, Lucky braced her hands on his chest, her fingers pressing into the smooth skin, layered over hard muscles. Her legs straddled one of his massive thighs and she couldn't breathe, nor did she want to.

If she died there and then, so be it. The kiss was everything she'd never expected, but suspected could be possible. The precise reason she'd avoided it in the first place.

Her blood turned hot, racing through her veins, her heart hammering against her chest and a delicious ache built down low, where her crotch rubbed his thigh. She moved just a little, and the friction of his jeans against hers sent shock waves through her nervous system. She moaned, her fingers clutching at him in an attempt to drag him closer.

What felt like only a moment or maybe a lifetime passed before he raised his mouth enough she could suck air into her lungs.

"Holy hell," she groaned, her body plastered to his like a

woman desperate to get naked. And oh, how that thought made her hot all over again.

"Holy hell is right." His fingers tightened at the back of her head, threading through her hair. "Who knew there was passion beneath the denim and cowboy hat?"

Warm breath feathered across her mouth and her lips parted. "That wasn't supposed to happen."

"But it did." His lips brushed across hers in a feather-soft caress.

She shivered with desire so strong it scared her. Sanity crept in and Lucky pushed against his chest. "It did, but it won't again. It can't." It would be wrong to kiss both brothers, wouldn't it?

"Wanna make a bet on that?" He let go, his eyes smoldering, sexy and completely mesmerizing. If she were the type of girl who could be easily mesmerized.

"I don't gamble," she said, her resistance wavering.

"Because you know you'd lose." He held out his arms. "I'm in your hands, nurse."

She retrieved the bandages, ointment and alcohol pads from where she'd dropped them on the ground, shoved them into his hands and backed away. "I think you can handle it from here."

"Won't you feel a huge sense of guilt if I contract lockjaw because I couldn't reach one of those on my back?" He gave her a poor-me, sad-puppy look.

Her eyes narrowing, she counted to ten then snatched back the items and went to work on the puncture wounds, less than gentle in her application of the alcohol.

"Sheesh! Go easy," he said.

"I should have come out here alone. None of this would have happened." And she wouldn't have been tempted by the brother of the man she'd made love to the night before.

He captured her hands. "Never work the ranch alone."

"I know, I know. Buddy system."

"Right." He let go, his hands drifting down her sides to her hips, steadying her while she applied ointment and bandages to his wounds. "You're pretty good at that."

"It's not rocket science." She patted one last bandage in place and stepped away.

His hands fell to his sides and he stood.

Tall for a woman, she felt short and feminine next to Trent who was at least another five inches taller than she was. She had to look up to stare into his eyes. Those deep brown, bottomless, soulful eyes. "You and your brother have the same chocolate-brown eyes," she commented.

"Is that so?" He frowned. "That's about where the similarity ends."

"You can say that again."

His frown deepened. "What do you mean?"

"You don't kiss anything alike."

"What the fuck?" He grabbed her wrist. "You've kissed my brother?"

She shrugged. "Maybe. But then that would be my business, not yours."

"It damn well is my business."

"What I do with my lips is my business alone." She planted her fists on her hips. "Why don't you stay here and let me finish the fence?" she said.

"Because it goes faster with two. As long as one isn't wrapping the other in barbed wire and kissing the other's brother."

Guilt washed over her. "I'm sorry. That was careless of me."

"The barbed wire? Or kissing Isaac?"

"The barbed wire."

Trent glared and touched one of the bandages, exaggerating a painful grimace. "If you feel that badly, I'll let you kiss my booboos tonight after I've had a shower." He waggled his brows.

Lucky glared and turned away. She refused to be caught up in his teasing and got back to work, careful not to cut a strand of wire without holding on to the loose end and then easing it to the ground. Four of the old wooden fence posts had rotted. She pounded two of the metal posts into place and Trent pounded the other two. By the time they'd finished stretching the wire with the come-along, the sun was beating down on them and they'd worked up an honest sweat.

"Are you hungry? Or would you prefer to cool off first?" Trent pulled his shirt on over the bandages, leaving it unbuttoned.

She pushed loose strands of her long straight hair back off her damp face. "Cool off." Thinking the ride back to the barn on the back of ATV would do the trick, she climbed on, not really wanting to press her sweating body against his.

When he goosed the throttle, she was once again forced to hold on or fall off the back. He turned the vehicle and headed a different direction than the one from which they'd come.

"Where are we going?"

"To cool off," he shouted over the engine.

That same feeling of dread and titillating anticipation filled her. This was going to be a very bad idea. With her hormones raging and her arms clinging to him, she tamped down a moment of panic. What if she couldn't resist him?

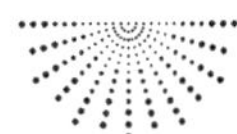

CHAPTER FIVE

Trent raced across a pasture to a copse of trees in a valley and pulled to a stop beside a widening in the creek, the old swimming hole he and his brother spent the better part of each summer splashing around in.

He'd forgotten how clear the water was and how the trees leaned over to shade the area from the harsh sun.

Lucky climbed off the back and stared at the water, then closed her eyes and inhaled deeply, her lips lifting at the corners. "I don't see how anyone could *not* like living here. It's full of treasures. It's beautiful, diverse and filled with everything a person could want. Wide, open fields and plentiful sources of water for the horses and cattle."

Trent studied her. Her eyes were bright, face flushed with exertion and sunshine. "Do you always think in terms of what's good for the animals?"

"I love working with ranch animals. I've done it my whole life." She glanced over at him. "But it's more than that. You have everything here. Fields for hay, wildflowers, the smell of honeysuckle, and sky for as far as you can see. What's not to love?"

He looked again at what she saw. He hadn't noticed the orange petals of the Indian blankets tipped in yellow, or the scent of honeysuckle clinging to the remnants of an old fence post. Nor had he remembered how clear the skies were in the summertime and the way the shade dappled the smooth surface of the water.

It took seeing it through Lucky's eyes to remind him of the magic of the Texas landscape. All he'd remembered was how much he resented his father's heavy hand raising him and how quickly he'd escaped as soon as he was old enough.

Yet here he was. Back on the ranch.

His jaw hardened. His plan was to stay only as long it took to convince Isaac to sell. Then he'd cut all ties with the home he'd never felt was a true home.

Now he was here with a woman who had made him hotter than the Texas sun. With a pool full of cool water in front of him, he wouldn't mind taking their kiss a step further. But he wouldn't push it, not when she worked for him. Still, he was hot, the pool was inviting and he wanted it. Trent reached for his belt buckle.

Lucky's eyes widened. "What are you doing?"

"I don't know about you, but I came to cool off. You can stand there and watch, or join me. And just so you know, this is what we do on the ranch. When we work hard in the heat, we come here to cool off. It has nothing to do with the fact you're a female. As far as I'm concerned, you're the ranch hand. Nothing more." He toed off his boots. Enjoying her flustered expression and the way her eyes darted from the boots to where his hands worked the belt loose.

"But your bandages…" she argued.

"Will probably fall off and likely have to be replaced. Better yet…" He reached up and plucked all the little bandages off, stuffed them in his pocket and grinned. "Now you don't have to worry that I'm polluting the pool with garbage."

"You could get an infection."

"The pool is spring-fed and that's a chance I'm willing to take." He unzipped his jeans and pushed them over his hips. He didn't wear underwear and they slid right down his legs, his cock springing free.

Lucky spun, giving him her back, her breathing becoming labored. "You could have warned me."

"It's much more fun watching you blush. Again, you're welcome to join me."

"I knew that kiss was a mistake," she muttered.

"So noted." He stepped out of the jeans and laid them across a bush. Then he waded into the water up to his waist. "You don't know what you're missing."

"I'll wait on the four-wheeler."

"Hey, loosen up. It's only water and I promise not to touch you if you don't want me to."

She glanced over her shoulder at him. "Why should I trust you?"

He frowned. "Because when a Jameson gives his word, he doesn't go back on it." That was one of the lessons his father had drummed into him early on. A promise was a promise.

She turned and faced him. "Do you promise not to look?"

"If it makes you feel better, I'll turn around while you strip." He swished his hand in the water. "It really does feel good. And you can wash the dust and sweat off."

Her gaze fixed on the water, her tongue sweeping out across her lips. "The water does look cool."

"Feels even better." He shook his head. "Suit yourself. I'm swimming away if you want to get in while my back is to you." Trent turned and swam slowly to the far side of the pool.

Moments later, he heard a splash. When he twisted around, he noted her jeans and shirt lying on top of her boots, but he didn't see her.

Then she surfaced, water streaming over her face and shoulders. She remained low in the water so her breasts were covered.

What she didn't know was that the water was so clear, he could see the tips of them easily.

His member hardened and he fought to keep his promise and not touch her if she didn't want him to. The challenge was to make her want him to. Cupping his hand, he splashed water her way.

"Hey!" She whacked the water, sending more his way. The fight ensued, Lucky giving as good as she got and exposing a lot more of her body in the process than she had probably thought.

Suddenly, she ducked beneath the surface.

He could see the outline of her body swimming beneath the shadow of a tree, and she disappeared. When she didn't come up right away, Trent tensed. Had she gotten hung up in some roots or vines? He turned, looking for her, and was about to duck beneath the surface and start a search when something grabbed his ankle and dragged him under.

He went down. A hand pressed against the top of his head and he sank deeper, but not before he caught his attacker around the hips and pulled her with him.

They surfaced together, gasping for air.

"You promised not to touch me." She braced her hands on his chest.

"All bets were off when you touched me first." He held her clamped to his body, her breasts smashed against his chest, her clean fresh face dripping with water. She didn't need makeup, she was naturally beautiful and deliciously wet, completely and undeniably desirable.

Trent was lost. He couldn't let her go.

Lucky stilled, her breathing rapid, her gaze on his lips. Her tongue darted out to swipe across her mouth.

"You make me crazy when you do that," he grumbled.

"Do what?"

He leaned in and swept his tongue where hers had been. "That."

"Umm." She cupped his face. "Let me get this straight. Did you mean this?" She tongued his lip, tracing the seam and then cocked her brows. "Or this?" Her mouth closed around his bottom lip and she sucked on it.

His cock hardened, nudging against her belly.

When she let go of his lips, he kissed her, his tongue sliding the length of hers, caressing, tasting and teasing. Then he released her mouth to skim the long length of her throat, angling toward one of those luscious breasts.

"Oh my." Her breathing became more ragged as he captured a nipple between his teeth and nibbled gently. "This isn't what I hired on for."

"Consider it one of the benefits of the position."

"I'm not that kind of girl," she said.

"I never thought you were." His breath warmed her damp skin.

Her fingers clutched his head, holding him against her while his mouth ravaged her areola.

A long, slim leg curled around the back of his thigh, skimming over his ass to hook around his waist.

"Just so you know," she whispered, "I don't normally have sex with my bosses. I've always been considered one of the guys."

"Oh, honey, you're anything but one of the guys." He pulled her breast into his mouth and sucked hard.

Her back arched, pressing her deeper and her head lolled back. Skimming his buttocks, her other leg came up around his waist, her ankles locking behind him. "Damn, that feels good."

"I have more skills."

"I'm sure you do." She moaned. "We shouldn't do this. I have work to do."

"It can wait." He backed her to the rocky ledge at the side of the pool and hiked her bottom onto it, parting her legs so that he could position himself between them.

"Really, we should be going." Her gaze dropped to where his cock jutted out in front of him as he stood up to his thighs in the water. She bit down on her lip. "Then again, it *is* lunchtime."

"I'm hungry, how about you?" He stepped closer until his cock nudged her opening.

"Starving." She gripped his hips and held him back. "But not too hungry to forget precautions." Closing her eyes, she dragged in a ragged breath. "Please tell me you have something."

He leaped out of the pool, grabbed for his jeans and fished in the back pocket for his wallet. "Damn!"

"What do you mean, 'damn'?"

"I mean, damn!" He tossed his jeans to the ground and lowered himself into the pool, his face tense. "I didn't bring my wallet. I usually don't when I'm working on the ranch."

"Damn," she agreed. "Guess lunch is over."

"Not so fast." When she started to clamp her legs closed, he pressed her knees wide. "Just because I don't have protection, doesn't mean this is over."

She shook her head. "It was a bad idea anyway. It's going way too fast."

"That's okay, if both parties agree, right?" He slipped lower in the water, his fingers trailing along the insides of her thighs to her center. "Technically we wouldn't be having sex. Or at least I wouldn't be getting off. But that doesn't mean you can't."

Her brow puckered as his finger dipped into her channel.

A quickly indrawn breath let him know he had her attention. "I could stop now…" He dragged his wet finger over her clitoris in a long, slow swipe that had her biting hard on her bottom lip. "…or not."

She whimpered. "Don't."

He removed his finger from between her folds. "Don't?"

Her hand closed around his and she slid his finger along that nubbin of her desire. "Don't stop now."

"Honey, that's just the beginning." He bent to apply his tongue where his fingers had been moments before.

LUCKY LEANED BACK on her hands, spreading her legs wider. Never before had she let a man do what Trent was doing to her in the open air. Never before had she been intimate with two men in less than forty-eight hours.

Maybe she'd been holding back too long. Perhaps all her troubles began with the fact she was so resistant to change she hadn't been flexible enough to let go and see what happened.

With slow deliberate strokes, Trent took her with his tongue, dipping into her channel, swirling around in her juices and rising to her clit with tiny, potent flicks that set off a rush of heated sensations, winging through her system, knotting in her core.

She lay back, unable to support herself on her wobbling arms.

"Like that?"

"Yessss."

A long lick from the bottom of her slit up to her tip of her nubbin had her crying out, her body writhing. "Please."

"Please, what?"

"Please, don't stop," she screamed.

Trent attacked her, his tongue laying siege to her senses, sending her skyrocketing into the stratosphere, somewhere above the treetops, in the bright blue Texas sky. She floated with the clouds, her muscles drawn up tight, her mind bound for the moon.

When at a last she fell back to earth, she lay as limp as a wet rag, incapable of movement or coherent thought.

"Like that?" Trent stood, his cock resting between her legs, rubbing gently across her swollen clit.

He grabbed her hands and sat her up.

"I don't have any bones," she said, slumping against him, resting her face in the crook of his neck. Running a hand across his chest, she trailed it lower to the hard erection jutting above the water. "But what about you?"

"I can wait."

"Does it hurt?" She circled his cock with her hand, running it down the base and back up to the tip.

He sucked in a deep breath on a hiss. "Not much."

"Let me take care of it." She slid her hand along his length.

"That's okay. You don't have to."

She slipped from the ledge and dropped down, the cool water surrounding her, barely reducing the heat of her body. "But I want to." Bending, she took his cock into her mouth. "Like this?" Her tongue snaked out and tapped the tip of his member.

It jerked and his belly tightened, the muscles standing out in that fabulously rigid six-pack.

"Is that right?"

"You have no idea how right it is." He twisted his hand in her hair and urged her back over him.

Wrapping her lips around the end, she sucked him into her mouth, reveling in the spring-water freshness with a hint of musky male. Damn, he tasted so good and the hard girth of his cock in her mouth only made her even hotter, sparking the same surge of desire in her core as his tongue had.

Lucky gripped his hips and urged him deeper into her mouth, dragging her teeth across his thickness.

When he bumped against the back of her throat, he pulled back.

Again, she put pressure on his hips, curving her hands around to the swells of his tight, beautiful ass. She started by setting the pace and soon he took over, pumping in and out of her mouth, his hands buried in her hair, twisting it tight.

The slight pain only increased her desire. He thrust faster and faster, until she forgot to breathe and thought she might pass out.

Then he yanked free, come squirting out over her breasts, warm and thick.

She gripped his member in her hand as he throbbed his release.

"Wow," he said, when he could speak again.

Now that their passions were spent, Lucky smiled shyly. Not knowing what else to do, how to bridge the awkward gap, she dove into the water and swam several feet away before surfacing.

He was beside her, reaching for her, pulling her into his arms. "You're not getting away that easily."

"I thought we were done," she said, her body still tingling where he held her against his.

"Far from it." He traced a finger from her cheek downward over her collarbone to where her breasts bobbed in the clear water.

"Nobody's ever done that to me in the open," she admitted.

He yanked his hand away and looked up at her. "You've never done it in a creek?"

"No." She chuckled. "I've just never…experimented… outside a bedroom."

"So you've been with a man?" he asked, his thumb circling her nipple.

She hesitated, then answered, "Mostly my fiancé."

"You mean your ex-fiancé, right?" Trent laughed. "Was he a prude?"

Like a cold slap, reality flung itself at her and all the bad memories rushed in. "No." She pushed against him and swam several steps away, covering her breasts. "I'd better get dressed. I shouldn't have done this." Her heart hammering in her chest, guilt rushed in to replace the desire of a moment before. "I can't do this. It's not right." Her throat constricting, tears welling in her eyes, she left the water, grabbed her clothes and ran up the bank.

Trent followed, completely uninhibited by his nakedness. He grabbed her arm and spun her around. "Holy hell, Lucky, are you still engaged? Should I expect a fiancé to appear out of the blue?"

She stared up into his eyes, her bottom lip trembling. "No. He won't appear. He's dead."

CHAPTER SIX

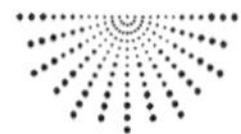

*T*rent drove back to the ranch house at a sedate pace so that Lucky wouldn't fall off the back. She'd insisted on walking back, but he wouldn't let her. The compromise was to go slowly enough she wouldn't have to hold on to him.

He still didn't understand why she was so upset. They'd almost had sex. She was single, free to make her own choices and no one held her back.

Then why was she so upset by what they'd done?

It had all changed at the mention of her fiancé. Her *dead* fiancé.

As soon as they pulled up in the barnyard, Isaac emerged from the barn. "There you two are. I was about to ride out and check on you. Was the fence that bad?"

"No." Lucky leaped off the back, grabbed tools, the roll of barbed wire and hurriedly entered the barn without another word.

Isaac's gaze followed her. "Was it something I said?"

"No." Trent didn't feel like talking, nor did he feel like

owning up to his little tryst with Lucky in the pool. It just wasn't any of Isaac's business.

Isaac wasn't letting him off that easily, following him to the shed at the back of the barn where they stored the ATVs. "What did you two do?" He dropped down beside the tires and whistled. "You took her to the creek?"

Trent fought a groan. "Yeah. So?"

Isaac straightened and crossed his arms. "Did you make a pass at her?"

"It's none of your business."

"I hired her. That makes it my business." His eyes widened. "Fuck, Trent. You did her, didn't you?"

"Keep your voice down."

"The hell I will. I want this ranch hand to stick around. And didn't I tell you earlier that *I* liked her?"

"And I've want to sell this hell hole from the beginning. It's nothing but work, and my *paying* work is falling behind."

"Then sell me your half. You needn't have anything to do with the ranch or anything else, including me, ever again."

"You know I can't do that. Terms of the will specifically say we both have to sell or neither can sell. If you agree to sell, I'm on it. I've even had an offer."

"Fuck you, Trent. This is my home. I'm staying. If you don't like it, get the hell out."

"You can't handle the upkeep on your own and you need my help. This place doesn't make enough money to support paying more than the two ranch hands and one is out until his knee gets better. You *need* my help."

"*You* don't want the ranch."

"I guess that leaves us at stalemate." Trent dug the

remaining tools out of the ATV's toolbox and stomped away.

"Damn right it does." Isaac called out after Trent, "And don't think I'll ever sell. You might hate this place, but I don't."

Trent stopped, turned around and glared at his brother. "You said you'd give it a year and if I still wanted to sell, you'd consider it."

"I've considered it." Isaac crossed his arms. "I don't want to sell."

Trent spun away, trudged to the house, kicked off his boots and stripped as he walked down the hall. A shower ought to clear his brain sufficiently to let him get to work on the project he'd been commissioned for.

Another oil rig to be placed in the Gulf. As if they didn't already have enough. This would be his tenth rig and, frankly, he was tired of it. He hadn't gone to school to be an architect to spend his life as an oil rig specialist. Back in college, he'd had dreams of building beautiful museums, something that combined his love of history, art and mathematics. Not something that destroyed the environment and littered the floor of the gulf.

He'd gone into the field straight out of Texas A&M, working with some of the best architects in the industry. He'd worked his way up the ladder until he was designing rigs on his own. Why? To prove to his father that he didn't need him. That he could make it on his own, without the ranch, without him, without putting up with his negativity.

As he stepped into the shower, he realized his fists were knotted.

His father was dead. He'd died almost a year ago, without ever telling Trent he was proud of him and all he'd accomplished.

Then why the hell was he still pushing himself?

He turned on the water, leaving it on cold, the drops pelting his body and all the tiny puncture wounds he'd accumulated when he'd been wrapped in barbed wire.

An image of Lucky's shocked face came to mind and he laughed, forcing his anger out. Yeah, he'd been mad about being wrapped in barbed wire. But when she'd stood beside the pool, staring around in wonder, he'd gotten a glimpse of a new perspective.

I can't see how anyone could not love this place, she'd said.

But he didn't love it. He despised it and every moment he'd had to work on it with his father telling him all the things he did wrong, never giving him a lick of encouragement.

If he hated it so much, why was he there? He had an apartment and office in Houston.

He'd told himself he was there because of Isaac.

One full-time foreman and Isaac only part time could not run a ranch this size. The ranch wasn't making enough money to hire more help, thus the reason he'd moved home when his father had died. Isaac needed his free labor to help out, especially when he had to be away for his regular job as a geologist for oil speculators. Trent figured that even having the competent help of another experienced rancher wouldn't be enough. Especially one with a long, leggy body that wrapped around a man's like it was his second skin.

His cock twitched, rising at the thought of plunging deep into Lucky's body. What would she feel like sheathing him? Warm, wet and wonderful, no doubt.

After the abrupt end to their lovemaking, Trent wondered if he'd have a chance to find out. The water wasn't cold enough to chill his desire. He had to have her, the blowjob not nearly satisfying enough to shake her from his thoughts. Once with her ought to be enough to get her out of his system. Once usually did it for him with most women he had sex with.

When he stepped out of the shower, he dried off and dressed in clean jeans and a soft chambray shirt. He padded barefoot into his father's office, sat at the desk and powered up the computer.

He spent the rest of the afternoon working on the *Limitless 11*, the latest in his patented designs. With his computer screens set on the intricate details of the structure, he worked without stopping, his mind going back and forth from girders to girl thighs until the smell of smoke drifted in through an open window.

"What the hell?" He leaped from his desk and ran out the French doors onto the deck. Smoke was coming from the other side of the house, the breeze wrapping it around the porch. He raced to see where it was coming from.

As soon as he rounded the corner, a wall of smoke billowing from the kitchen window hit him. Shouts and curses accompanied the clatter of pans from within.

Trent burst through the door. Smoke engulfed him, blinding him, making his eyes sting and clogging his lungs. He ducked low and spied jean-clad legs too slender to be his brother's. "Lucky?"

"I tried to tell you I was…" cough, "…hopeless…" more coughing, "…in the kitchen. I can't…see to turn off the… damned burner."

Crouching below the heaviest smoke, Trent raced across the floor and groped for the knobs on the stove, shutting off the burner.

Red-hot flames rose from a skillet, the smoke puffing out from there.

Trent grabbed a pan lid from the drawer in the bottom of the stove and threw it over the flames. Within seconds, the fire was out and the smoke began to recede.

"What the hell happened?"

Lucky staggered out the door onto the deck, doubled over and coughed like she was expelling a lung.

Trent pulled a glass from the smoked cabinet, rinsed it, filled it with water and joined Lucky on the deck, handing her the glass. "Drink."

Isaac came running from the barn. "What happened?"

"Good question." Trent's gaze turned to Lucky whose coughing had slowed, though her face was smudged with soot. "Mind cluing us in?"

Her brows pulled together and she brushed a lank strand of hair behind her ear. "I told you I was hopeless in the kitchen."

Before Trent or Isaac could say anything, she turned and ran for the barn.

Isaac glared at Trent. "What did you do to her?"

Trent raised his hands. "I was working in my office. Hell, I didn't know she was in the house until I smelled smoke. I thought she was in the barn with you."

"She was, at least until I rode out to bring that sick heifer in."

"Did you get her in?"

"Lucky?"

Trent's jaw tightened. "No, the heifer."

"Got her in the last stall in the barn. Got a call out to the vet. He said he might not make it until morning."

"How's she look?"

"Lucky? Hotter than hell." Isaac grinned at his brother, then his grin faded. "The heifer, not so good. Not sure she'll make it until the vet gets here."

"Damn." Trent hated losing even one of the animals. His father would have kept better track of the cattle. He'd have checked every other day on the herd, if not every day.

Another reason they should sell the ranch. They weren't cut out to be ranchers. They had other work demanding their attention, Trent's work as an architect and Isaac's work as a geologist.

"When are you due to head back out in the field?" he asked.

"Not for another week. Then I'm off to Montana." Isaac glanced at the house. "I hired her. I'll take care of the mess in the kitchen. You check on the cow and see if there's anything you can think of."

"Dad always took care of the sick animals. Anytime I tried to help, he refused. Said I'd do more good by getting Dusty out there to help him. He was too stubborn for his own good."

"Yeah." Isaac shoved a hand through his hair. "And Dusty's not here to help."

"It's probably not a good idea to call him." Trent scratched his five-o'clock shadow. "The man's probably pumped up on morphine or some other painkillers."

"Wouldn't be right to bother him." Isaac glanced at his brother hopefully. "Would it?"

"No." Trent tipped his head toward the barn. "I'll go see what I can do to make her comfortable."

"What do you want for dinner?"

"Something not burned."

"Frozen pizza?"

"We had that last night."

"Frozen chicken wings?"

Trent sighed. "We need to sell this place. I miss the restaurants in Houston."

"And the smell of oil refineries?" Isaac's lips thinned. "I'm not selling."

"You get to escape every other week."

"We can hire more help."

"Damn right. I have deadlines I can't miss."

"Saving the world one oil rig at a time?"

"Maybe. At least I'm trying to help make this country less dependent on foreign sources of fossil fuels."

"So noble." Isaac bowed, his whole attitude reeking of sarcasm.

"Don't knock it, you're in the same business, finding oil for speculators."

"Yeah, but you have a talent for building things. It doesn't have to be oil rigs."

"Oh, go cook something." Trent stomped off to the barn, his brother's taunt hitting far too close to home. After the brightness of the Texas outdoors, the interior of the barn was dark and filled with shadows.

He stood for a few moments, allowing his sight to adjust to the darkness.

Then he heard Lucky talking.

He followed the sound to the last stall where the heifer lay on her side, breathing hard.

Lucky crouched on the ground beside her, smoothing a hand over the animal's neck.

He must have made a noise, because Lucky glanced over her shoulder, her gray eyes rounded, sad. "She's dehydrated."

"The vet's coming in the morning."

"If we don't get fluids in her, she might not make it through the night."

"There's only one large-animal vet in the county."

"Then we have to do something." Lucky pushed to her feet. "Where are your supplies?"

"In a cabinet in the tack room."

"Show me."

Trent led the way, and Lucky followed him.

"Do you keep salt, potassium chloride and calcium chloride?"

He stared at her. "I have no idea."

She frowned.

"What? My foreman usually handles ordering supplies for the animals and takes care of any sick ones."

"You own the ranch."

"Yeah, but I didn't ask for it."

"That doesn't make sense."

"Inheritance from my father. The only thing he ever gave me."

She tilted her head, a smile playing at her lips. "I detect resentment."

"Yeah."

Her smile disappeared and she brushed him aside. "I don't have time for it," she said, her voice brusque, no-nonsense. One by one, she went through the cabinets until she located a box of salt and two more with calcium chloride and potassium chloride. She pulled them down onto a counter and then reached for the metal tube lying on a shelf above.

"What are you doing?"

"Saving that cow's life, if I can."

"You've done this before?"

"I told you, I worked on a ranch. I'm good with animals. That heifer is dehydrated. If we don't get her hydrated, she might not be around for the vet in the morning."

Curious now, he watched as she measured amounts of

the three ingredients into a clean bucket. "How do you know she's dehydrated?"

She rolled her eyes his way as if to say any idiot would know if they had worked around cattle much. "Her eyes have receded." Once she had the ingredients in the bucket, she filled it with water and stirred. "If you'll bring that tube and pump, we can get started." She didn't wait for him.

Trent grabbed the lid for the bucket that had a pump affixed to it, the tubing and nose pincher and hurried after Lucky.

She'd set the five-gallon bucket of liquid to the side and was herding the cow out of the stall and out the back door of the barn into the small corral. She didn't stop until she had her in the chute with the neck clamp. Quickly, efficiently, she situated the heifer in the clamp and held out her hand for the nose pincher with the short gray tube attached.

Trent handed her the items she asked for and observed while she worked on the heifer, shoving a longer tube through her mouth and into her belly. Soon she had the concoction she'd stirred up pumping into the heifer's stomach.

"Are you sure this is what you do?" he asked, remembering his father and Dusty doing something like this when he'd let Trent near enough to watch.

"I've done it more times than I remember. I grew up on a cattle ranch in the panhandle. I was drenching cows at the age of nine."

An hour and five gallons of liquid later, they moved the heifer back to the stall, gave her food and water and closed the gate. In that time, Trent had a whole new respect for the ranch hand they'd hired and it had nothing to do with how beautiful she was or how sexy she looked naked. Though that helped.

"She should be okay until the morning when the vet comes." Lucky brushed her hands on her jeans and sighed. "The horses have been fed. Tomorrow I'll check hooves and teeth. Is there anything else you want me to do?"

"I think you've got everything under control." He had to admit he was surprised by her expertise and hard work. He hadn't known many women…make that *any* women who could have done what she had that day. "You're amazing."

She snorted. "Except for the K.P. detail." Her head hung. "My father raised me to work the ranch, but he didn't bother to teach me to cook."

"I gathered that." He jerked his head toward the house. "I smell something that isn't smoke. Isaac isn't bad at the grill. Wanna go see what he's prepared?"

She glanced down at her dirty jeans. "I need a shower. Then I'm headed to the Ugly Stick. I have to work off the damages from last night."

He frowned, not too happy about having her work all day then late into the night at the Ugly Stick. "I can give you a ride."

"I appreciate that, but I'm not certain how late I'll be. I'd prefer to take my own truck."

"I don't mind. I was going there anyway, after dinner," he lied. The more he was around her, the more he found himself wanting to be around her.

She trudged toward the house, biting at that full bottom lip. "All right. But I'll drive my truck."

He glanced at the old pickup. "Will it make it there and back?" He didn't relish walking home in the middle of the night. "I really don't mind driving."

"Then *you* drive, but I'm taking my truck."

"We'll take your truck." Biting back a grumble, he held the door for her as she entered through the kitchen. He hadn't planned on going to the Ugly Stick, but now that he'd committed, he couldn't take it back. Besides, after a full day working the ranch, Lucky had to be tired and shouldn't drive herself home alone.

"Took you guys long enough. The steaks are getting cold."

"Where'd you get steaks?" Trent asked.

Isaac's chest puffed out. "Found them in the back of the freezer."

"I can't eat until I've had a shower." Lucky glanced around the kitchen.

Isaac grinned. "I did the best I could with cleaning up. A coat of paint will take care of the rest."

"I could pick up a can on my way through town, if the hardware store is still open." Her face fell. "On second thought, I will when I have some money in my pockets."

"We have some ceiling paint in the barn," Isaac offered.

"I can paint the ceiling tomorrow." Lucky glanced from Isaac to Trent. "Unless you want me to do it before I go to the Ugly Stick. I can, you know." She started for the back door. "In fact, I think I should. It'll cut down on the smoky smell."

"No!" both Trent and Isaac said at once.

Her eyes widened. "I don't mind. I created the mess, I should have cleaned it up."

"We don't mind, do we, Isaac?" Trent said.

"Hey, speak for yourself. I had to toss the pan and use steel wool to get the charred remains of a pork chop off the stove."

"I'm sorry." Lucky chewed that lower lip again. "Maybe

it would be best if I moved on. My bad luck seems to be following me, even here."

Trent slipped an arm around her shoulders. "I'd say you have a knack for more than that." He glanced at his brother. "You should have seen how she took care of that heifer. What did you call it?"

"Drenching." She shrugged. "Any ranch hand could have done it."

"No, I don't think so." Trent nodded toward the hall-way. "Do you have extra clothes?"

"Yes."

"Where?"

"In the back room."

Trent glanced over her head at his brother.

"I put her in the spare bedroom last night."

She'd slept in the house the night before and he hadn't known it. His cock twitched. And if he had, what would he have done? Stayed up all night wondering what she looked like naked?

"I don't expect to stay in the house long. Just until I can earn enough money to rent my own place."

"We don't mind your staying here, do we, Trent?" Isaac shot him a pointed glare.

"Not at all."

Lucky stood straight. "I don't take charity unless I have to." She shot a glance at Isaac. "And I plan on paying you back that forty dollars, as soon as I can earn extra money."

"You work here now. Your quarters are provided as part of the payment package."

"Do you have a bunk house?"

"No. Only the foreman has his own small house on the property."

"Then I'll find a place to stay in town."

"Don't be stubborn, Lucky." Isaac slipped an arm around her shoulder. "What if one of the animals needs you in the middle of the night? Trent and I are hopeless. We've had no training in animal husbandry."

"Isaac's right," Trent added. "It's either we pay your rent in town, or—"

"—you can stay in this house. We have three extra bedrooms. You might as well use one."

Her brow furrowed and she chewed on that darned lip again, making Trent want to take over and taste it himself. "What's it gonna be?"

She sucked in a deep breath and let it out. "Okay. But only until I can earn enough to pay my own rent. And don't tell me you'd do the same for a male ranch hand."

Trent smiled. "Actually, we would. Isaac and I have jobs other than ranching. We need the help and we'd pay for and put up with someone who can take care of things when we can't. And today, you've proven that you can more than take care of the ranching duties."

"All that said, it helps that you're prettier than a toothless cowboy." Isaac clapped a hand on her shoulder. "Go get your shower. You're staying here."

Isaac watched as she walked away, waited until she was out of earshot and then turned on his brother. "What the hell are you doing with Lucky?"

"What do you mean?"

"She hasn't been here an entire day and you've already had sex with her in the creek?" Isaac crossed his arms. "I saw her first. I was the one who hired her to work at the ranch. I want to date her. Did you think of that?"

"Seems to me you had your chance already. When did you have time to steal a kiss from her?"

"I didn't steal it. She gave it free and clear." He glared at his brother, wanting to tell him that he'd had sex with Lucky, but he wasn't one to kiss and tell. It was up to Lucky to share that information. Apparently, she hadn't. "You have a crappy reputation with women. What happens when you get tired of her? If she fancies herself in love with you and you don't return her feelings, our ranch hand will pull up stakes and leave."

"So?"

"Didn't you hear me? I want her for me. She's just the kind of woman I pictured myself with for the long haul. Kind, independent, hardworking."

"Beautiful, sexy and with legs that go on forever?"

"That too." Isaac stabbed a steak with a fork and slammed it onto a plate. "Don't run her off like you do every other woman."

"If she'd wanted you, don't you think she'd have shown it?"

She had and they'd done it. Isaac clamped down on his tongue to keep from saying that. "I was giving her a chance to get used to the idea of me and her."

"You snooze, buddy, and you lose." Trent slid one of the charred steaks onto his plate, spooned a helping of microwaved baked beans next to it and set it on the table.

Isaac placed the last steak on another plate and set his and Lucky's plates on the table, a jar of steak sauce and two glasses of ice water. "I'm not done yet. But you're right. I'm playing it safe. I think I could be the right guy for Lucky."

"And I'm not?"

"Hell no. You aren't stable enough. She needs someone who will care for her always."

"She needs someone who can stir her passion."

"I got this."

Lucky entered the room with her hair up in a towel, her face scrubbed clean. "You two didn't have to wait for me. Dig in." She sat, lifted a fork and knife and polished off the steak like a true ranch hand.

Yeah, no dieting, stiletto-wearing, frou-frou woman with more hairspray than brains. Lucky was the real deal.

Isaac studied her and his brother as they ate in silence. Tonight he would step up the pace on his goal to woo the fair Lucky into committing to him. He had more charm in his little finger than Trent had in his entire body, and he cared about Lucky. That his brother had taken her in the creek had him scratching his head. Was Lucky like so many other women and preferred the bad boy to the boy next door?

Well, hell. He could be just as bad as the next guy. Lucky wouldn't know what hit her. Isaac went after what he wanted, and he wanted Lucky for his own.

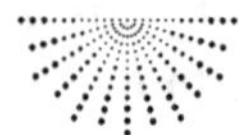

CHAPTER SEVEN

*L*ucky drove to Temptation on her way to the Ugly Stick Saloon with Isaac and Trent crowded onto the front bench seat beside her. She couldn't convince them that she was used to doing things on her own, and they insisted they were going to the Ugly Stick anyway. Right. Two nights in a row. They didn't strike her as big partiers.

Her truck might not be the newest, cleanest, best truck on the road. It coughed black smoke and the engine was sluggish when it started, but it was hers. She didn't have much left from her life growing up as the daughter of a ranch foreman. When her father had died of cancer four years ago, he'd used up all his savings on doctors' bills. All he'd had to leave her was the old truck.

"Since you're going to be early at the Ugly Stick, could we swing by the grocery store? I need razors and shaving cream," Trent said. "Anything you need, Lucky?"

She needed shampoo and something besides the harsh soaps the men used, but she refused to ask. It would be one more thing she'd need to pay back. At this point she was quickly becoming an indentured servant with the IOUs she was racking up. "No, thank you."

She parked out front of the grocery store and got out.

"Are you coming in?" Trent asked.

"No. I thought I'd spend the time checking out the town."

He snorted. "That won't take long."

Isaac hooked her arm with a charming smile. "I can show you around if you'd like."

The man was hard to resist when he smiled like that. "That would be nice."

Trent grunted, glared at his brother and entered the grocery store by himself.

Isaac proved to be a good tour guide, mentioning the historic buildings, the shops along Main Street, and he gave her tidbits about the people who owned them.

Small, quaint and homey. A community she could grow to love.

In the center of town, they passed a beauty salon called the Shear Safari, decorated like an African savanna with lions, giraffes and water buffalo painted on the windows. A woman waved from inside.

Isaac paused and waited for her to emerge from the salon.

Lucky recognized the woman as Mona, one of the two tipsy women who'd witnessed her knocking Audrey's truck into the ditch.

"Isaac, honey, who've you got there?" Mona hooked her arm through Isaac's and smiled all friendly-like at Lucky.

Lucky felt a little stab of anger at the way the woman clung to Isaac. Not that she was jealous or anything. After all, she'd almost made love to the man's brother in a pool earlier that day. She had no claim over the Jameson men.

Warmth spread over her breasts and up her neck. Wow. She got hot just *thinking* about them.

Isaac waved toward the woman dressed in leopard-print Lycra stretch pants. "Lucky Albright, this is Mona Daley, our resident beautician."

"Cosmetologist," Mona corrected, and held out her hand.

Lucky shook her hand and shifted in her cowboy boots. For the first time ever, she wished she could wear girlie clothes and do her hair like Mona's.

"How's Grant doing on the Rafter R since his retirement?" Isaac leaned close to Lucky. "Grant was the best bronc rider on the rodeo circuit until he quit this past year."

Lucky relaxed. Apparently the woman had a man.

Mona gushed, "He's lovin' every minute of it. Although when the rodeo comes back to town, I'm sure he'll be itching to ride. I know *I'm* loving it. I get *my* itch scratched a lot more often with him at home." She smiled again at Lucky. "So are you as lucky as your name?"

Lucky stiffened. "No." She looked away, the pain of too many people hating her for her bad luck rushing in on her. "It was nice meeting you. If you'll excuse me..." She crossed the street and walked back toward the truck.

A large, lanky, spotted hound dog darted out of the gap between the real estate office and the hardware store and ran right in front of her with what looked like a hunk of charred meat in its mouth.

A woman wearing tailored slacks and sporting gray-blue hair ran after the dog, shaking a long, wicked-looking two-pronged fork at the animal. "Stop! Thief! I'll kill that dog. I swear I'll kill it." She stopped, bent double and wheezed, then gathered herself and ran again.

Lucky didn't like the livid look on the woman's face. She followed, sure the dog would outrun the woman, but worried in case it didn't.

"Wait up, Lucky!" Isaac called out.

Lucky couldn't. If the dog slowed, the woman would skewer him like a kabob.

"Come back here, you bandit, you poor excuse for a canine," the woman yelled.

The hound ducked down an alley between buildings on Main Street, crossed a street, then slipped through a gap in some hedges.

"I've got you now," Crazy Lady screamed. "You can't get away from me."

Run, dog, Lucky urged. She glanced over the top of the hedges at the backyard of a three-story home with Grecian columns and an Olympic-sized swimming pool. The dog stood beside the pool, tearing at the meat, gobbling it as fast as he could, his ribs sticking out of his sides.

Lucky's heart went out to the dog. He was hungry.

The woman pushed through the hedges and waved her fork at the animal. "Now I have you. You won't be stealing food anymore." She stalked the dog, marching across the pristine lawn, murder in her eyes.

"No!" Lucky couldn't stand back and let it happen. "He only did what he had to."

"He's stolen his last steak." The woman jabbed with her fork as she backed the dog into a corner where the pool took a ninety-degree turn to a deeper end.

"Mrs. Rutledge, what are you doing?" a man called out from a window on the second floor of the home.

"I'm killing this dog," she said.

"No, you're not." Lucky raced around the woman, blocking her path to the hound. "He doesn't know he was wrong. He's thin, he's hungry and he's only trying to survive."

"He's a stray and should be put down. I'd be doing the town a favor."

"I won't let you." Lucky crossed her arms. "He's not a stray…" She glanced behind her at the dog that continued to tear into the thick steak, swallowing huge chunks whole. "He's *my* dog."

"Then you can pay me for the steak he just consumed."

"I will." How, she didn't know. But she wasn't letting this woman kill a dog someone had tossed out on the streets to die.

Mrs. Rutledge held out her hand. "I'm waiting for my payment."

"I don't have any money."

"Then move aside." The woman advanced, poking the fork at Lucky.

Lucky swung her arm up in one of the moves her father had taught her to defend herself against unwanted advances from randy men. She knocked the woman's hand away. The fork flew from her fingers and she teetered on the edge of the pool.

Oh no. Lucky lunged for her, but missed her hand, bumped her arm and sent her the rest of the way over.

The older woman hit the water with a huge splash and sank like a rock.

Lucky slipped off her boots and dove in after her.

Mrs. Rutledge kicked, thrashed and couldn't seem to find her way to the surface.

Her eyes stinging from the chlorine, Lucky grabbed the woman from behind, hooked her arm over her shoulder and under the opposite arm and surfaced, bringing her head above water.

Mrs. Rutledge gasped and fought, making them sink below again.

As Lucky surfaced, she spoke in a firm, calm tone. "Stop fighting it. I've got you. I'm going to swim to the shallow end. Stop fighting."

As if she hadn't heard a word Lucky had said, she continued to kick and struggle. Lucky managed to swim to the shallow end. "It's shallow here. Put your feet down."

"I can't…swim!" Mrs. Rutledge said, her eyes wide, scared.

"You don't have to. Put your feet down. The water is only waist-deep."

"Can't swim," she muttered, her feet drifting to the bottom. Once she had them under her, she scrambled for the edge, Lucky holding her arm the whole way.

Once she'd climbed up the steps, she collapsed into a lounge chair, dragging in deep breaths and coughing out the water she'd sucked into her lungs.

An older man with gray hair and clear blue eyes ran out of the stately mansion. "Mrs. Rutledge, are you all right?"

"I am, no thanks to this fool!" She pointed her finger at Lucky. "She tried to kill me."

"No, she didn't." Isaac pushed through the hedge. "Dang, woman. I wouldn't have found you if not for all the ruckus." He faced the older man and nodded. "Judge Stephens, I got here just in time to see Lucky drag Mrs. Rutledge *out* of the pool."

"I wouldn't have needed to be dragged out of the pool if she hadn't pushed me into it." Mrs. Rutledge waved her finger, her lips curled back in a snarl. "She tried to drown me, knowing I couldn't swim."

"No, ma'am. I didn't," Lucky retorted. "It was an accident."

Mrs. Rutledge pulled herself up to her full height, dripping wet. "Judge Stephens, be so kind as to call the police. This woman should be arrested."

"Now, Barbara. I witnessed most of what happened from my library upstairs."

"Then you saw her knock me into the water. You can bear witness to her assault."

"I didn't assault her," Lucky insisted.

"From what I saw, Barbara, you were waving a sharp object. I'm sure she was only defending herself."

"Defending herself? Against a woman of sixty-seven? Like I could harm anyone." She curled up on the lounge, making herself look older, feebler than the crazed woman of moments before threatening to kill a helpless dog.

"She was going to kill that dog," Lucky said.

"Isaac?" Trent burst through the hedges into Judge Stephen's backyard. "I heard you were in some trouble. Where's Lucky?" His gaze swept over the two wet women and he did a double take. "Mrs. Rutledge? Lucky? What's going on?"

A police siren wailed into the neighborhood and stopped somewhere on the other side of the huge mansion.

Lucky moaned. *Not again.* Why couldn't she just live a quiet life? One where people weren't quick to judge or place blame.

A sheriff's deputy rounded the side of the mansion and was almost knocked over by the frightened hound that'd finished his dinner and knew when to hide.

"Catch that dog! He's a thief!" Mrs. Rutledge screamed. "And arrest this woman. She attacked me."

The deputy took out a notepad and pen. "Now, Mrs. Rutledge, please explain to me which one was the attacker and which one was the thief."

"You idiot, you let the dog get away. Call in animal control."

"Ma'am, we don't have a separate animal control. I'm your animal control officer as well, and since there is only one of me, which thief or attacker would you like to catch most?"

"Her!" The older woman pointed at Lucky, and then shifted her finger to where the dog had disappeared. "No, catch the dog! He stole Mr. Rutledge's dinner."

The deputy glanced around. "I'm sorry, but it seems the animal has disappeared."

While the deputy took stock of the premises and checked behind bushes, Lucky stood. "I have to get to work."

"Hold on just a moment, young lady. You're as guilty as that mangy dog." The woman pushed to her feet and poked a finger in Lucky's chest. "Arrest her."

"On what grounds?" the deputy asked.

"Because I told you to." Mrs. Rutledge shook her finger at the young deputy. "Billy Joe Frazier, don't make me call your mother."

"Ma'am, my mother is on a cruise in the Caribbean. I'm sure she'd love to hear from you."

"Don't smart-mouth me, young man. Arrest that woman. She's a threat to the community."

The deputy sighed and glanced at Judge Stephens. "Sir, did you see what happened?"

"I did."

"Did this woman shove Mrs. Rutledge into the pool?"

The judge frowned. "Well, now. I saw Mrs. Rutledge shaking something at her and the next thing I know, Barbara's in the pool."

"See? She tried to kill me."

The judge frowned and continued, "The young lady dove in after her."

"To make sure I stayed under," Mrs. Rutledge lied.

"She sank like a stone," Lucky said. "I went in to get her out."

"I'm sorry, Mrs. Rutledge, it's your word against hers. And since you're not dead and the judge saw her pull you out, I'll have to let her go."

"That won't stop me from filing charges."

The deputy tucked his pad and pen into his shirt pocket. "You have that right, ma'am."

"I'm calling my lawyer as soon as I get home."

Trent stepped forward. "Mrs. Rutledge, be reasonable."

The old woman turned on him. "Don't 'Mrs. Rutledge' me." She shook her finger at Trent now. "You could have my daughter, Stefanie, by just asking. Instead you and your no-account brother hire a woman to do who knows what out at the ranch. Why your father would be rolling over his grave, God rest his soul."

Trent glared at the woman. "Ma'am, that was rude and uncalled for. Apologize to Miss Albright."

"I'll do no such thing. She's nothing more than a tart, a tramp and a bad influence on the God-fearing citizens of this town."

Lucky winced. Is that what folks thought? That she'd been hired on for other than ranch work? "I'm not a whore, Mrs. Rutledge, if that's what you're suggesting."

"Whore, floozy, call it what it is. You're being paid by these men."

"To work the ranch." Lucky stepped up to the woman. "Not for sexual favors." Those, she'd given away freely.

"You have no right to attack Lucky like that," Isaac said.

"Why not?" Mrs. Rutledge looked down her nose at Isaac. "*She* attacked *me*."

The deputy stepped between the older woman and Lucky. "Mrs. Rutledge, let me take you home before this escalates further. I can give you a ride in the back of my car."

"Darn right you will," the older woman muttered, squeezing the excess water out of the hem of her blouse. "And when we get there, my husband will have words with you."

"I'm sure he will." The deputy nodded toward Lucky. "I wouldn't go too far. I'm sure you'll be called back into court."

"Great. That would just make my day." Lucky glared at Mrs. Rutledge, unwilling to back down when the woman had impugned her honor. "At least she didn't kill the dog."

"I'll have that dog destroyed, first chance I get." Mrs. Rutledge tapped the deputy's arm. "I'll be callin' the sheriff as well."

"Oh yes. The dog." The deputy drew in a breath and let it out. "I'll have a look around once I get Mrs. Rutledge home safely."

"When you find it, you can put the mangy mutt down," the cranky older woman said. "If you don't, I will."

Trent shook his head as the deputy walked Mrs. Rutledge around to the front of the house. "That woman has a mouth the size of Texas."

Isaac touched Lucky's arm. "Don't let her get to you. They were only words."

"But if she's thinking them, who else is?"

"No one else that matters," Isaac assured her.

If enough people thought the same, she'd be right back in Comfort, being shunned and run out of town for something she never did. Her hope to start over had taken a bad turn, and just when she'd begun to like Temptation.

The hound dog that had started the commotion slinked out from under a bush.

"There he is," Lucky whispered.

"Here, boy." Isaac inched toward the dog.

Lucky called out softly, "Don't scare him and don't let Mrs. Rutledge hear you."

"Got it." Isaac squatted on his haunches and held out his hand. "Come here, boy. You don't want that mean old lady to find you first."

Lucky grinned. Isaac waited patiently for the dog to come to him.

After several long moments, the animal crawled on his belly to touch Isaac's hand with his nose.

Isaac moved carefully, slipping his hand along the dog's snout to scratch his ears.

The hound rolled over, exposing his belly for a rub.

"Such a vicious creature, aren't you? I can see why Mrs. Rutledge took a dislike to you." Isaac scratched the proffered tummy. "This your dog, Judge Stephens?"

The older man shook his head. "Not mine."

"Want him?" Trent asked.

"I'm away too often," the older gentleman said. "I couldn't spend the time with him."

"What are we supposed to do with him?" Trent asked.

"He needs a good home where he can get lots of exercise. A big yard to play in." Lucky's lips twisted.

"Oh no. You're not bringing that dog back to the ranch. I'm trying to *limit* the number of animals. And we don't know if he'll try to eat the ones we already have."

"It's that or have him euthanized." Lucky ran her hand

along the animal's bony rib cage. "Which would be better than starving to death, but…"

The dog licked Isaac's face with a long, wet tongue.

Isaac looked into the dog's face. "You don't hold any punches, do you?" He glanced up at his brother.

"No. Not no, but hell no. He's not living at the ranch. He'd chase the cows, eat the chickens and terrorize the horses. No."

Lucky's mouth pressed into a tight line. "He's hungry. Nobody wants him and he has nowhere else to go." Kind of like she'd been yesterday. The correlation too close to home. Her heart squeezed hard in her chest. She couldn't ignore the dog's situation. Everyone deserved a home and to be loved. This dog was no different. She looked to Trent. "Please."

WHEN LUCKY LOOKED at him like that, with those big gray eyes and all the hurt and sadness rolled up into that one word, Trent's automatic *no* froze on his lips. He stalled, asking, "Why us?"

"You have a perfect place for him," Lucky explained.

Trent crossed his arms. "Yeah, and what happens to that dog if we sell that place?"

Lucky shot a glance between Isaac and Trent, her brow furrowing. "Are you really selling?"

Isaac tipped his head toward his brother. "He wants to, but I have to agree to sell, or it's not happening. I'm not selling."

"We'll see," Trent said, though he'd been leaning the other way the more time he spent with Lucky. The image of her naked body, seared into his memory, still made his blood burn.

Isaac scratched the hound's belly. "How can you put a dog down that rolls over for a tummy rub? He reminds me of that stray you brought home when I was ten. Whatever happened to that dog?"

"Dad took him for a long walk with his shotgun." Trent's gaze rested on the malnourished canine, his jaw so tight a muscle twitched. "He's dirty, he smells and he probably has fleas."

"I'll give him a bath as soon as we get back to the ranch," Lucky promised.

"You still have to work at the Ugly Stick. What are you going to do with him while you do?"

"Maybe Audrey will let him stay in the storeroom. Or he can stay in the cab of my truck after sunset."

After a long pause, Trent sighed. He'd always wanted a dog, but his father never let him have one. And it did remind him of the stray he'd brought home when he was twelve. That dog had never had a chance with his father. This dog didn't have to meet the same fate. "Fine. We'll take him home. But the first time he eats a chicken, he's gone."

"He won't eat a chicken if we feed him properly." Lucky flung her arms around Trent's neck and hugged him, pressing her body against his. "Thank you. You won't regret it."

His hand resting around her waist, he stared down into Lucky's shining eyes, his heart skipping several beats when the thought struck him. She felt right in his embrace and her happiness made him feel better. Better about *what*, he wasn't sure. Maybe it was that her happiness rubbed off on him.

"Come on, dog, you have a new home." Isaac lifted the

dog and carried him toward the hedge. "He needs a name. Trent, you call it."

"I don't care."

"Oh, come on. Every dog needs a name."

He thought back to the name he'd given the stray, not knowing his dad would take him out and shoot him later. "Otis."

Lucky nodded. "I like it. Otis it is."

With Lucky in the driver's seat and Otis sitting all over Isaac's lap in the center, Trent could just imagine what they looked like driving down Main Street in Temptation. Since he'd left Temptation, he'd worked hard at polishing his image, pulling himself out of the country-boy upbringing. Driving around town in a beat-up truck with a mangy hound dog didn't fit the image he strove to display. Still, he couldn't help the smile.

Otis turned to him and swiped his face with a long, wet tongue.

Trent didn't even mind that.

Too bad Old Lady Rutledge hadn't witnessed it. She'd have had a conniption fit. Trent hid a grin at the thought. He'd seen the hurt in Lucky's eyes when Mrs. Rutledge had called her a whore and had felt a stab of guilt for coming on to her in the pool, though he couldn't begin to regret it.

She'd woken in him something he thought long dead.

Need. Hunger. Desire. A fresh view of the world. Coming home had been a dark pall in his life.

Lucky was making him see it differently.

She'd only been in his life for a day. A single day. Having appeared out of seemingly nowhere, he was almost afraid she'd disappear as easily. And suddenly, he realized he didn't want her to.

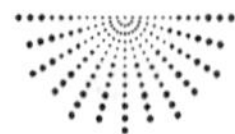

CHAPTER EIGHT

*D*espite her side trip to rescue a stray, Lucky managed to arrive as the Ugly Stick Saloon opened. The Jameson brothers entered through the front door while Lucky parked her truck in the back. Otis seemed content to sleep on the seat. As soon as she found an old bowl, she'd bring him some water.

The night before had been Ladies Night. With it being Friday night, the bar was already filling up with cowboys getting off work and ladies looking for fun. The sun had set, the band was tuning up and it looked as if it would be a good night for sales.

"I'm so glad you came back." Audrey carried a box of full whiskey bottles to the bar and placed them one at a time on the shelf. "Two of my waitresses called in sick, so I'm short staffed."

"I've never waited tables, but I'm willing to give it a shot."

Audrey eyed Lucky's jeans, cowboy boots and chambray shirt. "Normally my waitresses wear cut-offs and tight tank tops. It's part of the draw to the Ugly Stick

Saloon. The cowboys expect it."

Lucky glanced down at her jeans. "These are my best jeans, I can't cut them off."

"I think I might have something in the prop room that'll fit you. Come with me." Audrey led the way to the backstage area where Lucky had run into Cory McBride, one of the strippers from the night before. The room was empty, the costumes and props neatly shelved or hung on racks.

Audrey sorted through one of the racks and pulled out a dark leather vest. She set it aside and found a pair of faded blue jean cutoffs and held them up to Lucky. "These might fit. Try them on."

"Here? Is there a changing room?"

Audrey laughed. "Honey, this is the changing room. And believe me when I say, you don't have anything different than I've already seen. I bought this saloon on money I earned stripping."

Lucky gulped. "I've never stripped in front of…"

"A woman?"

"I was going to say a stranger." Lucky fiddled with the button on her jeans. "But other than my female doctor, I've never stripped in front of a woman either."

"If it helps, I'll turn my back." Audrey spun toward another rack. "Go on. We need to get out there before the cowboys start hollerin' for their drinks."

Quickly, Lucky toed off her boots and dropped her jeans, glad she'd worn a decent pair of bikini panties, her one concession to her feminine side. As quickly as she'd shucked her jeans, she slipped on the pair of cutoffs.

Lucky buttoned and zipped. "They're tight and really short."

Audrey turned back holding a bright, red-white-and

blue bikini top. When she spied Lucky, her face lit up. "Well, look what was hiding behind men's blue jeans."

Lucky's face heated and she covered her ass with her hands. "I can't go out there in these. My butt is showing."

"Honey, all my waitresses' butts are showing just a little. You'll get used to it."

"I don't know."

"Trust me, they look good." Audrey handed her the bikini top and vest. "Now take off your blouse and bra and put these on."

Lucky crossed her hands over her breasts. "I can't."

Audrey shook her head. "You're working to pay off your debt right?"

"That's why I'm here."

"Don't you want to earn a little more cash to tide you over?"

Lucky nodded.

"You'll work off your debt by waiting the tables. Your tips are yours." She held up the red-white-and-blue bikini top and the dark vest. "You'll get more tips if you wear these."

"Are you sure?" Lucky took the items and answered her own question. "Of course you're sure. You've been in this business long enough you should know."

"So what are you waiting on? The sooner you get out there and wait tables, the sooner you'll get tips. Go, go, go!" Audrey headed for the door. "Wear the boots with the outfit. When you're done dressing, I'll show you the ropes."

Left alone, Lucky hurried out of her shirt and bra and dressed in the bikini top and vest. The top was tight, pushing her breasts up and out, giving her cleavage that made her face heat.

Audrey ducked her head back into the room. "One

more thing…" She entered carrying a brush, an elastic band and a handful of hairpins. "Let's get all that glorious hair up to show off that beautiful long neck."

Lucky wanted to protest that her neck wasn't beautiful, but Audrey took charge, pushed her into a chair and went to work. In less than two minutes, she had Lucky's hair pulled up on top of her head in a loose, messy bun with tendrils hanging down her back and beside her ears. She hauled out a bag of makeup and applied powder, blush, eyeliner and mascara to Lucky's face, topping it all off with a layer of pale pink lipstick and gloss.

When she was done, she planted her hands on her hips and studied Lucky. "Wow. Who knew a beautiful woman was hiding under those baggy clothes?" Then she clapped her hands. "Get your boots on. We have work to do." Audrey whisked out, leaving Lucky's head spinning.

Pulling on her boots, she jumped up and ran for the door, catching a glimpse of herself in a full-length mirror as she passed by. She skidded to a stop and gasped. The woman staring back at her didn't look anything like Lucky Albright. This person had long slender legs, a cute, rounded ass, tight abs and full, ample breasts. Hell, she looked like a model for one of those hot rod magazines the ranch hands used to keep under their bunks. The kind who sprawled across the hoods of shiny cars or straddled wicked-looking motorcycles.

Part of her wanted to cover her exposed skin. The vixen she'd only recently discovered on the Triple J Ranch was screaming *hallelujah*!

With an uncustomary giggle, she threw open the door to the prop room and ran smack dab into a hard wall of muscle.

Hands reached out to steady her and a familiar voice said, "Pardon me, miss."

When Lucky glanced up, she could actually see the moment recognition hit Trent Jameson.

His eyes widened, his nostrils flared and his fingers tightened on her arms. "Lucky?"

She felt a surge of power and pushed her shoulders back.

His gaze dropped to the swell of her breasts and heat flared in her core.

Schooling her voice to calm when her insides were rioting with desire and nervousness, she said, "Oh, hey, Trent, I was just on my way out to wait on tables. Is there something I can do for you?"

His wide eyes narrowed and his lips thinned. "You can put your clothes back on for one. And wipe that makeup off your face."

She stepped back far enough his hands dropped from her arms. When she tried to step around him, he moved to block her. "Please move. I'm working."

"As what?" he demanded. "What did Mrs. Rutledge call it?"

Anger roiled up inside her and, before she could think straight, she slapped Trent's face. "I let that woman get away with calling me a whore. But I'll be damned if I let you. I didn't have sex with you for money. This is my time off. I can do whatever the hell I please. So get out of my way."

"You can't go out there like that. Those men are animals."

She stood with her hands fisted on her hips. "And you're better than they are?"

He opened his mouth to say something, and then snapped it shut.

"Thought so." Lucky raised her brows, adjusted the vest over her top, exposing even more skin. "Now allow me to pass."

Trent stepped aside. As she marched by him, he grumbled.

Mimicking the models she'd seen on runway shows on television, she put one booted foot in front of the other, emphasizing the sway of her hips.

Take that, Trent Jameson!

As she neared the end of the hallway, she looked back over her shoulder.

His brows were drawn into a heavy frown.

Lucky tossed her head and stepped out, ready to face the crowd of rowdy cowboys and whatever they had to dish out.

And she walked right into one of the waitresses, carrying a loaded tray of full beer mugs, bottles and wine-glasses.

The tray flipped, the mugs tumbled off, crashing to the floor, some landed in a customer's lap, others broke into pieces when they hit the hardwood floor.

The man whose lap got the worst of it jumped, his chair tipped backward and he fell over onto a cowboy who had just risen to hit the dance floor. That customer went flying into the lap of a pretty woman with a big, burly cowboy date.

"Hey! That's my girl," Burly Boy bellowed.

Lucky watched in horror as the big guy lifted the other cowboy up by the scruff of his neck and slammed a fist into his face.

He flew backward, landing in the lap of yet another woman and the fight was on.

Men threw punches, women screamed and some lifted chairs to crash down over men beating up on their dates.

Audrey leaped onto the bar stuck two fingers into her mouth and whistled long and loud.

Burly Boy swung one last time, the guy he hit spun around and landed on Lucky, who staggered backward into Trent's arms.

"Who's here to have fun?" Audrey shouted. She nodded toward the seasoned waitresses who clambered up onto the bar in their cutoffs and boots.

A faded *Yeehaw* could barely be heard over the squeals of the electric guitars.

"Seriously? My girls don't dance unless they have your undivided attention." Audrey raised her eyebrows and asked, "Soooo… Who's here to have fun?"

A rousing *Yeehaw* shook the rafters. Cowboys and cowgirls alike clapped and whistled, straightening the chairs and tables and settling the woozy ones back in their seats.

The band struck up the tune to "Save a Horse, Ride a Cowboy" and the waitresses on the bar kicked up their heels and danced in unison.

While the dancers had the saloon's attention, Lucky hurriedly cleaned up the spilled beer and broken glass. Trent and Isaac helped, making quick work of the effort.

By the time the dancing was over, the saloon was in order and the band played "Cotton-Eyed Joe" to get everyone up and on the dance floor, even those with black eyes, busted lips and bruised knuckles.

The waitresses went back to work serving drinks, nachos and buffalo wings.

Audrey slipped up beside Lucky.

"Audrey, I'm so sorry. I was coming out to help and—"

She raised her hand, a smile tugging at her lips. "I don't want to know. I just need help out there on the floor. And try not to start a riot this time." She winked to take the edge off her words, then showed Lucky the set of tables she was to cover and left her to it.

The saloon owner could have shown her to the door and banned her from ever coming in again. But she hadn't.

Lucky fought an uncharacteristic rush of tears. She didn't deserve the second and third chance, but, by golly, she'd show Audrey she wasn't a lost cause, someone who should be thrown out of town because of circumstances beyond her control.

She liked it here, she liked her jobs and the two men who'd invited her into their house and onto their ranch. Damn it, she intended to make it her home.

TRENT SAT with Isaac at a corner table, nursing the same beer he'd ordered an hour before.

Isaac drummed his fingers on the tabletop. "You plan on sitting here all night?"

Trent nodded. "Yup."

"Expecting more trouble?"

"Yup."

"Why is it trouble seems to follow our Lucky?"

"Our Lucky?"

"I hired her."

"She's not a horse to be owned."

"If she was, she'd be a prize thoroughbred with those long, sexy legs." Isaac stared across the saloon at Lucky as she loaded a tray with beer mugs and wove through the crowded room, smiling and laughing at the customers. She wasn't as natural at the waitress thing as the other ladies, but she was making a good show of it. The cowboys liked her and she managed to get the orders right.

Twice she'd returned to their table to get their orders. Each time she'd blushed, her cheeks turning a pretty shade of pink beneath her tan.

Her all-American, girl-next-door look shined through the fancy hair and makeup Audrey had duded her up with.

"She looks so different from the ranch hand of a couple hours ago." Isaac grinned. "Damn, she's got killer legs."

A stab of something like anger ripped through Trent's gut. He knew she had great legs. He'd seen her naked in the swimmin' hole. And he wasn't sure he liked all the rowdy cowboys ogling those mighty-fine legs.

"I like her better without all the makeup," Trent mused.

"I don't know. She's pretty hot the way she's put together tonight." Isaac stood.

Trent sat up straighter. "Where are you headed?"

"Thought I'd stretch my legs."

Trent spied Lucky ducking into the back of bar that led to the rear exit. He pushed to his feet.

"Where are you going?" Isaac asked.

"Going to see a man about a horse."

Isaac shook his head. "I'll never understand how that saying came about."

"Guess it all depends on the horse," Trent said with a grin. "I'll be back shortly."

Isaac aimed for the dance floor while Trent ducked through the front entrance. He glanced up at the night sky. After the heat of the day, and the crowd inside the saloon, the cool night air and the sparkling stars above calmed him like it always did.

He didn't get these kinds of night skies in Houston. With the light pollution as bad as it was, he was lucky to see any stars from the windows of his apartment. That was one thing he missed most about living on the ranch. The sky.

Trent headed around the side of the saloon to the back where Lucky had parked the truck, pausing at the corner to observe her as she inched toward the vehicle, carrying a bowl of liquid that spilled a little with each step.

When she reached the truck, she hesitated.

"Let me help you." Isaac stepped out of the rear entrance to the bar.

"Oh, Isaac, good." Lucky tilted her head toward her right side. "My keys are in my pocket. Can you get them out and open the door for me?"

Isaac grinned. "Gladly." He came up behind her and stood so close, Trent's teeth ground together. "This pocket?" he asked. "I don't feel any."

Lucky giggled. "That tickles. I guess they're in the other pocket."

Before Isaac could reach into her other pocket, Trent stepped out. "Having difficulties?"

Lucky jerked, splashing water on the ground. "Oh, Trent. You startled me."

"I was just getting Lucky's keys out for her." Isaac reached for her pocket.

"Just the keys," Trent said in a low dangerous tone.

"Testy, aren't we?" Isaac chuckled and held up the keys. "What did you think I was after?" Isaac winked from behind Lucky's back and stuck the key in the lock and opened the old truck's door.

Otis leaped out and would have gotten away if Trent hadn't grabbed him by the scruff and said, "Sit."

As if he recognized the command in Trent's tone, Otis squatted, his tail sweeping the dirt.

"Hello, Otis. How's it going?" Lucky lowered to her haunches, placing the water bowl in front of the dog.

Otis lapped the water while Lucky unwrapped a napkin filled with slices of barbeque brisket.

Before she had it completely free of the paper napkin, Otis snatched the meat from her hand practically taking her fingers with it.

"Hey, big guy. It's okay. There's more where that came from." Trent removed his belt and slipped it around the animal's neck then led him to the grass on the edge of the parking area where the dog could do his business.

When he'd taken care of his business, Otis loped over to Lucky and sniffed her hands.

"Sorry, boy." Lucky scratched Otis's ears and stroked his back. "I have to get back to work. You'll have to wait to eat dinner when we get home."

Home. Something pinched hard in Trent's heart. Hearing Lucky call the Triple J Ranch *home* did something to him. He'd never really considered it home. Not since he'd left swearing he'd never return.

Lucky turned to go back inside.

Isaac captured her elbow and smiled down at her. "I'll walk you back."

They were halfway to the door when Lucky glanced over her shoulder. "Aren't you coming, Trent?"

With his heart squeezing tightly in his chest and his stomach knotting, he shook his head. "I wanted to get some air. I'll be back in a minute."

Lucky hesitated another moment, her eyes shining in the light from the corner of the building. "Don't be too long."

His gaze followed her until she disappeared inside the saloon.

Then he turned and walked away, out onto the highway and a half a mile down the road before he stopped. What was he doing?

The woman had burst into his world, upended his life like she'd upended the tray of drinks earlier that evening. Before she'd appeared, Trent hadn't really wanted to keep the ranch. After his father died, he'd wanted to sell it, get out of Temptation and resume his life in Houston as if coming back to the Triple J had just been a formality. Working with his brother had brought them closer, but he'd still straddled the fence about selling versus keeping the ranch.

Now he found himself saddled with a dog named Otis and a ranch hand who cared about a cow and didn't mind getting dirty and shoving a tube into its gut to keep it alive long enough for the vet to come in the morning.

She was as fresh as a summer breeze and as sexy as a blanket of stars spread across the sky, and Trent couldn't seem to get enough of her.

So why was he out walking the highway in the middle of the night?

Because she conflicted him. When he wanted to sell the ranch, she came along and pointed out all the reasons he couldn't. Zeroing in on the things he'd forgotten or pushed to the side with all the hurts and unhappiness he'd harbored from when he was younger.

He'd seen the ranch as a burden, she'd seen it as a wonderful place full of promise and sunshine.

Trent returned to the saloon at a much slower pace. What was he going to do with Lucky? He'd only known her a day and already he couldn't imagine the ranch without her. Or his life, for that matter.

He frowned. And his brother had walked her back into the saloon with his hand at the small of her back.

Picking up the pace, he burst into the saloon, his gaze scanning the crowd, searching for Lucky. She wasn't carrying a tray or serving drinks. Audrey was covering her tables.

Where the hell was she? And where was Isaac?

A loud laugh carried across the barroom from the dance floor. Isaac held Lucky in his arms, teaching her how to two-step.

Trent wove through the tables, leaped over stretched-out legs and finally made it to the dance floor where he tapped his brother's shoulder. "I'm cutting in."

"We aren't done." Isaac continued leading Lucky around the dance floor, leaving Trent standing in the way of the others.

He moved back to the edge and waited for the song to end. As the music wound to a stop, he was pushing his way through the couples to where Isaac and Lucky were laughing.

"I told you I was hopeless," Lucky said.

"You weren't all that bad, you just need more practice. It's like makin' love on the dance floor." His hand drifted lower on her back. "Wanna go another round?"

"I need to get back to work. Audrey shouldn't have to cover my tables."

"I was gonna ask if you'd like to have dinner some time." He cupped her cheek. "I'd really like that."

Trent chose that moment to bust in. "She's busy."

Isaac frowned. "I think the lady can answer for herself."

"I need to get back to work." She pulled free of Isaac's embrace and inched around Trent.

"You can go back after this song." Trent grabbed her hand and twirled her away from Isaac.

"Hey, we weren't finished," Isaac groused.

"Yes, you were," Trent shot back at his brother.

"Fine. I'll get a beer." Isaac stomped away.

"I didn't say I wanted to dance." Lucky tugged her hand free.

Trent refused to relent. "Good, because I didn't ask."

She stood in the middle of the floor, one fist propped on one perky hip, a toe tapping her impatience. "What's wrong with you? You've been cranky since I went on break."

He glared at her. "I'm not cranky. Are you going to dance with me or not?"

"Not. Especially when you put it like that. I work for you and your brother, but you don't own me." She pulled her hand free of his and turned to walk away.

He captured her arm and yanked her around, slamming her against his chest. "Please," he said through gritted teeth, his voice softening as he stared into her gray eyes and his insides melted. "Dance with me."

She looked up at him, the anger still there in the rigid line of her jaw. "Okay. But I have to warn you. I'm not any good." Her cheeks reddened as he wrapped his arms around her.

"You don't have to be." He leaned his cheek against her hair. "Because I'm very good."

She snorted. "I'll be the judge of that."

"Game on."

CHAPTER NINE

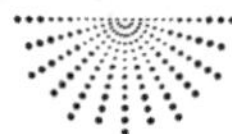

Though she tried to hold on to her anger, Lucky couldn't help melting against him, the feel of his body making hers turn to mush. "Cocky much?" she whispered, her lips so close to his neck she brushed them against his skin.

"Only with you," he said, his breath warm in her hair.

His hand rested against her naked skin at the small of her back, reminding her of how it felt to have him stroke her body with those work-roughened fingers.

"I meant to say thank you," he said.

"Really? I should be thanking you. I wasn't sure I was doing it right, considering that was my first time."

He leaned back and stared into her eyes. "I thought you'd said you'd done it since you were a child with your father."

Lucky's cheeks burned and she ducked her head, laughing shakily. "Oh, drenching the heifer. Yes, well, you're welcome."

"What did you think I was thanking you for?"

She dared to glance up, embarrassed by the direction of her thoughts.

"You thought I meant the pool." His hand tightened, pressing her against him and the hard ridge rising beneath the fly of his jeans. "Thank you for that too. Even more so."

Pressing her face against his shirt, she refused to look up at his laughing eyes. "Do you take all your women to the pool and do…that?"

He stopped in the middle of the dance floor and tipped her chin up. "For the record, I've never taken a woman to the swimmin' hole and I've never made love to one there."

She looked up into his eyes, hers seeming to see straight into his soul. "Technically, we didn't make love."

"A technicality I aim to remedy at the soonest possible occasion."

How would it be to make love to this man in a real bed? It had been pretty tempting on a rocky ledge and in the water. A bed with sheets against her back and the lights down low… A shiver of excitement rippled through her. Then she thought about who lived in the ranch house besides Trent. "What about Isaac?" He was sweet and seemed to really care how she felt.

Trent stiffened. "What about him?"

"I like Isaac." And she didn't want to hurt him. In fact, she was starting to have feelings for him. Especially those hot, wet sensations she got when she remembered how he'd made her feel the night before when he sank into her. He was the light to Trent's dark.

"Like, as in you think he's nice like a kid brother, or as in you'd like to sleep with him?"

She shrugged. "Like I think he's sexy and sweet, and he lives in the same house with you. And maybe…"

"*I* live in the same house. *I* want you."

"What if I don't want to choose between you two? Won't that cause friction between the two of you?"

His grip tightened around her. "I'm not sharing you with him, if that's what you're getting at."

"Up until I met you and Isaac, I never gave a threesome much thought. I've heard of such things, but I've always been one of the guys. All this getting naked in a swimmin' hole is new to me."

"You learn quickly." He rested his cheek against her hair. "And though you look really hot in those shorts, you look even hotter naked."

"That doesn't resolve the issue of your brother. You and I might only be a flash in the pan. Family is forever. I don't want anything you and I might do to come between you and your brother."

"I'll take my chances."

"How would you feel if I decided I liked your brother better?"

He leaned back and stared into her eyes, a frown pulling his brows together in a deep V. "Do you?"

"He's very handsome." She tipped her head. "He looks a lot like you."

"Are you tellin' me you like my brother better?"

"I don't know." She sighed. "I'm saying I think it's too soon to know either one of you."

"You know a lot more about me than you do him."

"Not necessarily."

"Does that mean you're going to sleep with him to get to know him better?" His tone and his jaw hardened.

"Contrary to what happened this afternoon in the pool, I don't play around with cowboys. I just think we're moving too fast."

"I don't think we're moving fast enough." He pulled her

against him, rubbing the hard ridge of his fly against her tummy.

Yes, he was excited. But lust was different than love. "What will happen when you get bored with me?"

"Who said I'd get bored with you?"

"You don't strike me as a man who stays with a woman for long."

"What do you know about me?"

"Not much. Again, that's my point." Lucky stepped out of his embrace. "I don't know anything about you. What we did this afternoon was completely out of character for me. This whole situation with you two isn't something I'm used to. Although all this attention is great, I'm still not sure it was a good idea."

"What the hell are you talking about?"

"Will you be mad if I decide I want a relationship with your brother after you decide you've had enough of me? Will it create hard feelings between the two of you?"

"Woman, you're talking in circles." Trent leaned his head back and pinched the bridge of his nose. "Why don't we discuss this tonight after you're off work?"

Lucky leaned into him and whispered in his ear, "Trent?"

He sighed. "Are you going to give me the brush-off now?"

Her eyelids drifted over smoky-gray eyes. "For what it's worth, I think you're good. Very good." She patted his chest. "As a dancer." She left him standing in the middle of the dance floor and went back to work, wishing the time would fly so that they could continue the discussion back at the ranch. She had a feeling the continuance would have little to do with talking.

To avoid staring at Lucky, Trent studied his brother as he tapped his fingers on the table.

Isaac's eyes narrowed, his gaze on Lucky as she wove through tables, carrying a tray of drinks. "What did you say to Lucky to leave her frowning?"

Trent scratched his head. "I'm not sure, but I think she wants to sleep with you to decide if she likes you better than me."

His brother's eyes lit up. "Really? Why didn't she say so?" He clapped his hands together, a grin spreading across his face. "After you two returned from fencing, I thought she'd never even glance at me again. I mean, you did it in the creek, didn't you?"

With his back teeth grinding together, Trent fought to keep his mouth shut.

Isaac slapped his palm on the table. "Good for Lucky!"

Confusion, frustration and anger bubbled up inside Trent. "What do you mean?"

"She's single, independent and intelligent. Why shouldn't she sample her options before she settles?"

"I'm not into sharing my woman with other men, even if the other man is my brother." He jerked a hand through his hair. "Hell, *especially* if he's my brother."

"You're kidding me, right? Are you really that uptight? I thought for sure living in Houston for the past decade, you'd have loosened up about sex. Welcome to the twenty-first century. Women are taking charge of their own sexuality. If they want to have sex with more than one partner, they can and will."

Trent didn't want to hear it. He lifted his beer and downed half of the warm brew before slamming the mug on the table. "I'm an old-fashioned kind of guy, and damned proud of it."

"I guess if you're into Lucky, you'll get over it. How will she know it's you she wants if she doesn't try out some others?" Isaac grinned and pointed to his chest. "Like me." His lips twisted. "Unless you're afraid she might like me better. Is that it?"

That was exactly it, and Trent didn't like that his little brother had nailed it before even Trent could figure out what had him so bothered. "I'm going out for some air. You coming?"

"No, I think I'll stay and keep an eye on Lucky. This night is becoming more interesting by the minute."

Trent lurched to his feet and headed for the door before he started a fight. And he really wanted to fight. Lucky had him tied up in a knot and he would dearly love to land his fist in a cowboy's face. Sadly, his brother's face was the one he most wanted to punch.

Lucky had a point about her causing a rift between him and Isaac. And Trent wasn't liking it one damned bit.

WHEN LUCKY HAD LEFT Trent on the dance floor, she'd been so conflicted, she could barely get her orders straight. Working for the two Jameson brothers was proving more complicated than she'd thought.

Her father had worked on the same ranch for nearly forty years without running into anything like this. He'd never been fought over by two owners or fallen for the owners. Hell, he'd never been attracted to the owners, that Lucky knew of.

He went to work each day, trying to make ranching turn a profit so that he could keep his job and a roof over their heads. Why did working on a ranch have to be so difficult?

If she had a lick of sense, she'd get back to the basics and concentrate on the animals. Animals were so much less complex than the humans who considered themselves superior. Ha! Humans were just plain messed up. Even she was confused, finding herself liking the role of an Ugly Stick Saloon waitress a little too much. For the first time in her life, she felt really feminine and she liked the attention. Maybe she wouldn't like it so much on a regular basis.

Before the saloon, she'd done her best to fit in as one of the guys. She realized she'd succeeded all too well. None of the cowboys she'd worked with on the ranch her father managed looked twice at her. In dirty jeans and cowboy boots with her hair pulled back and no makeup, she wasn't the most attractive woman in the county. If the number of butt pinches and ass slappings was any indication, some of the men here found her interesting, if not attractive. Now, she was considering asking Audrey if she could keep the shorts. For that matter, she had a really old pair of jeans she could cut off and fray. She had great legs. Why not show them off?

As the night neared its end, the crowd thinned and Audrey cornered Lucky at the bar. "You should go home and get some rest. I'm sure the Jameson boys have you up early with ranch duties."

"I rise with the sun."

The saloon owner's lips twisted. "Honey, that's just a few hours away. Go." She waved her hands. "Get some sleep. Or whatever else the boys have in mind."

Lucky's cheeks warmed. "What do you mean?"

Audrey's brows rose. "Honey, if you don't know what I mean… Oh hell, Lucky. If two extremely handsome men want to have wild and wicked sex with you, I hope you have the wherewithal to accept the invitation. It's not a sin to have two at once. It's a sin to pass up an opportunity like that." With a wink, she lifted a tray full of beer mugs and headed across the floor.

Her blood pumping hard through her veins, Lucky headed for backstage, where she located her blouse and jeans and slipped out of the vest and bikini top.

Two men. Holy hell. The image of both Jameson men making love to her at once had her blood burning. Standing almost naked among the racks of costumes, she could imagine what it must feel like to strip in front of someone. Deliciously naughty. And hadn't she already stepped out of her comfort zone once earlier in the day when she'd gone swimming with Trent as well as making love to Isaac the night before?

With cool air-conditioned air feathering over her breasts, her body heated. Audrey and Jackson had made love in the storeroom with her watching. *Knowing* she was watching. Had the pair also made love in the costume room?

With the costumes representing everything from cops to cowboys, a couple could play out any fantasy they desired. And here Lucky was fantasizing about doing just that. Her cheeks flamed and her pussy clenched.

Audrey hired out strippers for bachelor parties and adult birthday parties. Lucky wondered if she'd ever have the nerve to strip at a party? Would she be able to strip down to something as revealing as a G-string and pasties?

A riding crop hung from a nail near Lucky. When she plucked the whip from the wall, she shivered with a sexy, wanton delight, amazed at her ability to shed her former prudishness. Her time with Trent and Isaac had been a real eye-opening. And now that her eyes were fully open, she couldn't seem to get enough.

She fingered the crop, loving the feel of leather against her fingertips. What would it feel like against her naked body? What would it feel like to have a man trail the leather across her breast?

Lucky closed her eyes and dragged the end of the riding crop over the swell of her right breast, pausing at the tip, now distended and aching. Her pussy clenched, a rush of juices pooling low.

With a moan, she treated her other breast to the same, flicking the nipple with the end of the crop.

"Give me that," a deep, rich voice said and a hand wrapped around hers before relieving her of the crop.

Lucky's eyes flashed open and she stared into Isaac's dark brown eyes.

She covered her breasts with her hands. "What are you doing backstage?"

"Audrey said you could leave. When I couldn't find you outside or in the saloon, I figured you were back here." He grinned and drew her into his arms. "If I'd known you were into riding crops, I'd have been back here a lot sooner. Hell, we have an entire collection at the house."

"I'm not *into* riding crops."

"You're not? But I saw you doing this…" He traced the breast with the leather tip.

Lucky gasped and closed her eyes, her breathing arrested in her throat.

"Feel good?" he asked.

"Yes," she said, then opened her eyes wide, aghast at how good it felt to be in Isaac's arms, him teasing her body with the crop. "Where's Trent?"

"Here." Trent appeared, his angry gaze locked on Isaac. "What are you doing?"

"Lucky and I are playing show and tell. I'm showing her

how good a riding crop can feel, and she's telling me how much she likes it."

Lucky saw the storm brewing in Trent's eyes. Sure she'd made almost-love to him earlier the previous afternoon, but that didn't mean he owned her body. Audrey's taunting words replayed in her mind. *If offered the chance to have two men, take it.*

She offered her other breast to Isaac. "Do the other, please." She closed her eyes, inhaling deeply, her breasts swelling out. "Umm. That does feel good. You have a collection of riding crops, you say?" Lucky opened her eyes, her gaze on Trent's face.

He seemed to be struggling between rage and lust. "I thought we had something going."

Isaac let the crop drop to his side. "Lucky, if you and my big brother have something, I'll stop now."

She stared into Trent's eyes. The longer she paused, the darker the rage.

"We *almost* made love in the creek," she admitted.

Isaac stepped back. "But we...I won't come between you, if that's what you want."

Trent directed his anger at his brother. "Good, then go wait in the truck. Lucky and I have something to discuss."

"No, Isaac. Stay." Lucky straightened, anger pulling her up to full height. "I haven't committed to anyone, and as far as that goes, neither has Trent. He's free to pursue any woman in the bar or anywhere else for that matter."

He smacked his hat against his thigh. "I just might."

"Then go ahead. Isaac was treating me to the delights of sex with props." She pushed out her naked breast. "Continue, please."

Isaac glanced from her to his brother. "You okay with

this Trent? I don't mind if you stay and watch, if Lucky doesn't mind." He grinned. "It's kind of kinky."

"I'm not into kink," Trent said but didn't leave.

"Maybe you should consider it." Lucky guided the crop to her nipple. "Lower, please." Was this really the cowgirl who'd been too shy to get undressed to go skinny-dipping?

Isaac dragged the crop down her torso to the mound of hair hidden beneath her panties at the junction of her thighs.

Trent's breathing became labored. Like a bull in the ring, his breath exited his nose in hard puffs. He sounded like he wanted to paw the ground and charge.

"I don't know, Lucky, he looks like he might blow a gasket." Isaac cast glances toward his brother. "Maybe we shouldn't."

"Please," she entreated, her gaze locked on Trent's. "I've never had sex with someone else watching. It…intrigues me." She slipped her tongue across dry lips.

Trent ripped the crop from Isaac's hand. "If anyone's going to watch, let it be Isaac."

"Are you staking a claim?" Lucky asked.

"No."

She lifted her chin. "Then go away and let Isaac continue."

Isaac dragged the crop between her legs and across her pussy. "How are you for being spanked?"

Trent actually growled.

Lucky hid a grin. "I like the way you think, Isaac. But wait." She shimmied out of her panties, turned and pointed her ass at him. "I've always wondered what it felt like to be whipped." She winked at him. "Proceed."

Isaac went to strike her, but Trent's hand shot out and

snatched the whip from his hand. "I can't allow you to do that."

"Oh, come on, you don't think I would hurt her, do you?"

Trent glared. "I don't know what the hell to think." He slapped the crop against his open palm, the smacking sound making Lucky's pussy clench. Holy hell, would he spank her already? She'd stepped way out of her comfort zone this time and the longer the two men stood there, the more her confidence waned. Audrey had missed the mark on this pair of brothers. They weren't that into her, or into sharing her.

Lucky straightened, crossing her arms over her breasts. "Well hell, I loused this up too, didn't I? The riding crop and being in the room where all the strippers had been last night must have gone to my head. Now, all I'm feeling is embarrassed and extremely awkward." She grabbed her jeans and shirt and started to dress.

Trent reached out with the crop, laying it over the jeans as she started to jam her legs into them. "Don't."

"Don't do what?" she asked, heat rising up her neck into her cheeks.

Isaac cupped her cheek. "What he means is, the last thing we want is for you to feel embarrassed or awkward." His hand slipped over her arm and down to rest on her hip. "If having the two of us is what you want, I'm sure we can come to some agreement." He jabbed his elbow into Trent's gut. "Right, brother?"

Trent grunted, the riding crop pressing the jeans until she dropped them on the floor.

"What do you want from me?" she whispered.

"We want you," Isaac said.

"I believe you, Isaac." She nodded toward Trent. "I'm not so sure your brother knows what he wants."

"You." He set the tip of the crop on the side of her face then slid it down her neck and across the rise of her breast. "I want you."

"Enough to share with your brother?" she asked. "I refuse to come between you. And frankly, I like both of you. Isaac because of his charm and sincerity."

"And Trent?" Isaac's brows rose, his lips curling. "Surely not for his charm and sincerity."

Lucky snorted. "Hardly."

Trent's forehead furrowed. "Not funny."

"I like him for his animal passion."

It was Isaac's turn to frown. "You *know* I can be passionate."

Lucky grinned. "Yes, sir, you can."

Trent's face reddened under his tan. "You two did it?"

She nodded. "Got a problem with that?"

Trent opened his mouth, then snapped it shut without saying anything.

Lucky challenged Trent with a look. "Well?"

"Well, what?"

"As far as I'm concerned, I won't choose between you. It's all or nothing." She thought for sure he'd choose the latter option, leaving her high and dry and ready to plea-sure herself to relieve the ache in her core.

"I'm thinking." Trent's eyes narrowed, staring hard at Lucky as if to dare her to retract her ultimatum.

She didn't.

Isaac stared at his brother like he'd lost his marbles. "Really, Trent? This is a no-brainer. Lucky's a beautiful, intelligent, sexy woman. And at the moment, very naked. She's willing to have us both. I don't see the problem."

"I do." Trent crossed his arms. "I'm not into threesomes."

"And you speak from experience?"

"No."

"Then how do you know?" Isaac demanded.

Lucky raised her hand. "Forget it." She reached again for her fallen jeans. "I'll work for you, but I'm not choosing between the two of you." She almost got a foot into her jeans this time, before Trent stopped her again.

CHAPTER TEN

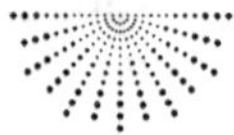

"*D*on't." Trent pressed the riding crop against her jeans.

"What my brother—" Isaac started.

Lucky stopped Isaac. "Let him speak for himself."

Trent's jaw twitched and Lucky thought he would turn and walk away. But then he said, "Don't get dressed." He plucked the jeans from her hands and tossed them to the corner. "If you want to be spanked, I'll do it."

"And Isaac?"

"He can watch. Or he can do whatever you want him to do."

"Will you..." Lucky pressed her hands over her distended nipples and swallowed hard on the rising wave of desire threatening to steal her breath away. "Will you both make love to me?" she whispered.

"Hell, yeah," Isaac said before Trent could speak.

Lucky waited for Trent's response.

Finally, he nodded.

Lucky let her hands fall to her sides. "I've never done this before, so I'm not sure of the logistics of a threesome."

"I have, and it's easy." Isaac grinned at Trent's frown. "What? I'm charming. But I'm no saint." He faced Lucky. "I call front. Which means Trent takes the backside."

Her cheeks burned with a mix between the lingering embarrassment and the heat of lust. She'd never been sandwiched between two men and the thought had her wet between her legs before they'd even touched her.

Isaac didn't waste time, he moved in to claim her breasts, his hand cupping the swells, weighing them in his palms. "Perfect." He bent to flick his tongue across one, while turning Lucky's back to Trent. "Don't just stand there. You have her permission to make love to her. Hurry before she changes her mind. Unless you want me to have her all to myself."

"All or nothing," she reminded him.

"Trent. I'm counting on you." Isaac ran his hand over Lucky's bottom. "Tell me you can resist that milky-white ass."

Trent groaned and reached out to cup her ass, squeezing the flesh, kneading it between his rough fingers.

"Still awkward," Lucky gasped.

"What's wrong?" Isaac asked.

"I'm the only one naked here. And what if someone walks in?"

Isaac waggled his brows. "We make it a foursome."

"No way." Trent leaned his cheek into Lucky's hair, inhaling the fresh scent of her shampoo. "I draw the line at three. And I wouldn't consider it at all if it wasn't my brother."

"Nice to be loved." Isaac pulled his shirt over his head

without unbuttoning. Then he shucked his boots and jeans. He stood before Lucky buck naked.

"Umm… Not bad." She touched his chest. "It's too bad your brother is so slow. You'll have a head start." Her hand circled Isaac's engorged cock and she caressed it from base to tip.

"Jeez, Trent. What the fuck are you waiting on?"

"My pride." He'd never been involved in a ménage. It didn't feel right.

"Fuck your pride. Lucky's worth a hell of a lot more than your pride. Show her how it's done."

Trent unbuttoned the top two buttons on his chambray shirt, got impatient with it and ripped the rest loose, buttons pinging off the walls. He toed off his boots and dropped his jeans, kicking them to the side.

Isaac spread a black cape out on the floor and dropped to his knees. "Come here."

Lucky joined him, easing down on her knees.

Trent followed suit. Parting Lucky's legs from behind, he moved in between them and smoothed a hand over her ass. Then he traced the seam between her cheeks to the smooth, tight hole of her anus and lower to the damp entrance to her pussy.

His cock twitched. He remembered what he carried in his wallet, and reached for his jeans. This time, he'd have the satisfaction of thrusting deep inside her. So what if his brother was there to watch. A trickle of excitement grew into a raging river of desire coursing through him, sending pressure to his groin, his cock swelling, growing, jutting forward.

Digging in his wallet, he found the little foil packet, ripped it open and rolled it down over his member.

Isaac kissed Lucky, his fingers threading through her

hair, drawing her closer as he thrust his tongue into her mouth, his hand gliding down over her torso to cup her sex.

Trent sucked in a breath, his muscles tightening. From behind Lucky, he reached around to cup her breasts, twirling the tips between his thumbs and forefingers. "Isaac is right for once."

"Hallelujah." Isaac released her mouth and trailed kisses along her cheek and down her neck.

Trent pressed a hand to the center of Lucky's back between her shoulder blades, easing her forward onto her hands and knees.

"Like this?" she asked.

"Yes." He slipped a finger into her pussy, then another, and another, stretching her entrance, dragging this wet fingers up to the anus where he poked his thumb into the tight little hole.

He bent to press a kiss to her ass. Her skin was smooth as silk and he rubbed his cheek against it.

Meanwhile, Isaac guided her face to his cock.

Lucky took him into her mouth. Seeing her swallow his brother's dick made Trent so hard he thought he'd come before he got inside. He remembered the way her lips had wrapped around him at the swimming hole, the way she'd held his balls in her hand, playing them between long, slender fingers.

Holy hell, he wanted her, but he wanted her to want him as much. His fingers slipped between her folds and he stroked her, flicking her clit until her back arched and she moaned around the cock in her mouth. Several more strokes and she tensed, her body going rigid.

One more long, stroke and a gentle tap on that little

nubbin of nerves and she cried out, her fingers digging into Isaac's hips.

Trent moved in from behind, positioned his dick at her entrance and thrust, long, smooth and deep. Her tight channel gloved him in warm wet heaven. The crop lay on the floor beside her, taunting him. She'd wanted one of them to spank her with it. Did he dare? He raised the crop and tapped it lightly against her flank.

Lucky flinched and moaned. "Again," she said breathlessly.

He smacked her again.

"Harder," she breathed.

Afraid he'd hurt her, he tapped just a bit harder.

"Harder," she begged.

This time he popped it, leaving a red mark on her pale white ass. Guilt made his hand freeze before the next pop.

"Yes!" she exalted. "Again!"

His cock hard as steel, he stung her with the crop.

With his hand holding her hips, Trent settled into a primal rhythm, thrusting and whipping, the combination sending him to the edge of orgasm, where he hovered near the peak.

His brother pumped from the opposite direction, his face screwed into an intense mask, his fingers threaded through Lucky's hair, urging her to take more, faster and faster.

One final thrust and Trent burst over the edge, catapulting into ecstasy.

Isaac called out, his dick buried in Lucky's mouth.

When Trent came back to earth, he pulled free, cupped Lucky's sex and smoothed a hand over her ass. "Wow."

Isaac chuckled and echoed his brother. "Wow."

Lucky collapsed on the cape and rolled to her back. "I don't think I have a single bone left in my body."

"Let us dress you and take you home."

"You'll have to." She lay there as they pulled her jeans up her legs, fingering her and touching her as they went. When they sat her up and pulled her blouse over her shoulders, Trent had to taste her nipple before covering them. Isaac too.

When they finally had her decent and had dressed themselves, Trent lifted Lucky into his arms and carried her to the truck at the back of the saloon.

He'd forgotten about Otis. The dog had no sense of timing.

When they settled a sleepy Lucky into the center of the seat, Otis clambered into her lap and lay down.

Lucky laughed.

Trent couldn't help laughing with her. Before long all three of them were laughing and the dog barked.

Trent drove them home. Lucky fell asleep, her cheek resting against his shoulder.

When he carried her inside, she didn't wake. Isaac turned back the covers, Trent laid her on the sheets and stared down at the woman who'd turned his life upside down.

"I want to do it all again," Isaac said.

Trent grunted. "Guess we'd better leave her to sleep."

"Would you do it again, if she asked?" Isaac asked.

Trent stared down at Lucky. "No."

"Still want her all to yourself?"

"Yes."

Isaac snorted. "You never were good at sharing your toys."

"Lucky's not a toy."

"Yeah, and you've never been able to commit for more than two days." Isaac brushed the hair away from Lucky's face. "I won't let you hurt her."

"Who said I would?"

"I know you."

"Maybe you don't."

"I'd sell the ranch before I let you break her heart. She's had it rough enough. She deserves a little happiness. Someone to love her just the way she is."

Love? Trent frowned. When did love enter into this equation? Lucky had only been with them for a little over a day. And already Isaac thought he was in love with her. How the hell did he know?

How could any man be that certain that soon?

Lucky was great, she was everything he'd always said he wanted. But was it enough for a happily ever after? His parents had promised to love, honor and cherish until death. His mother had left before Isaac's second birthday, leaving behind her two children and a man so bitter he never looked at another woman and seemed to blame his boys for their mother's disappearance.

Trent feared he'd be the same and drive away the woman he cared about. It was easier not to care than to die a cranky old man with no one to love or love him.

"She's just a girl." Trent glanced once more at Lucky, knowing in his gut he was wrong. She could possibly be *the* girl. But he had no intention of giving his heart and having it ripped from his chest. Better to leave it intact. "I just wanted the sex."

Isaac stared across at him, his face filled with disgust and disappointment. The disgust, Trent could take, the disappointment cut deep. He turned away.

"You were right," Isaac said. "I don't know you. And what I do know, I really don't like."

Isaac remained behind.

Trent left the room, stripped out of his clothes and showered away the scent of Lucky on his skin. No use getting soft. Guarding his heart had become an art form. Why let a cowgirl with an unlucky streak get to him?

Lucky lay awake into the wee hours of the morning, regret eating away at her. She'd been greedy to want to make love to both brothers. If she'd gone with her instincts, she'd never have made love to either and stuck to her farmhand roots.

The insanity of the Ugly Stick Saloon and daring to step outside the box that had become her existence, had led to her wrecking her chances at staying on the Triple J Ranch.

She'd been awake when the brothers had argued over her. She'd heard Trent's statement that he'd only been after the sex. That Isaac had stuck up for her warmed her heart at the same time as it chilled her soul. The men disagreed and she was the cause.

As she'd predicted, by sleeping with one or both of them, she was setting herself up with a ticket to leave. She'd rather remove herself from the equation than see the brothers argue over her.

After the veterinarian's visit the next morning, she'd pack her truck and head out, leaving her tips to pay back the money she'd borrowed from Isaac. Audrey had said she knew of an apartment that wasn't too expensive but it wouldn't be far enough away. No, she'd have to leave town.

She could send Audrey the rest of the money she owed when she found another job.

Otis padded into her room and lay down beside her bed. She'd take him with her. He was as unwanted and homeless as she was. They could keep each other company.

With a plan in mind, Lucky tossed and turned, drifting off into a restless sleep where Mrs. Rutledge chased after her with a meat fork and the entire town stood against her, asking her to leave. Thankfully, the wail of a wind rattling the panes of glass in the windows woke her from the depressing dream. Unable to settle back into sleep, she dressed, pulled on her boots and stepped outside in the early-morning darkness.

Wind whipped her hair into her face and not a star shined down to light her way. Clouds churned by wind hung low, smelling like rain that had yet to fall and quench the thirsty land.

Lucky crossed the yard, Otis bumping against her legs as she aimed for the barn. She felt her way around to the side door and switched on the light as she entered.

The horses whinnied and a sad moo came to her from the last stall. She hurried toward that sound, worried that the drenching hadn't been enough. Hopefully the vet would be there soon.

The heifer lay in the straw Lucky had filled the stall with earlier, her big sad eyes looking up at Lucky as she entered.

She squatted beside her and ran a hand along the animal's neck. "Hey, girl, the doc should be here soon."

Otis curled up in the straw and closed his eyes. Now that he had a place to stay and he'd been fed, Otis was perfectly satisfied. If only it was that easy to fall asleep.

Lucky wandered through the barn, searching for a

blanket. She found one in the tack room and carried it to the heifer's stall where she spread it out on the straw and lay down to keep the heifer company until the vet arrived.

The barn was big, well maintained and smelled earthy like horses, hay and leather. Like home. Too bad this would be the last day she'd spend in it.

She checked the heifer one last time and laid her head on the blanket, thinking back over the last few years.

Her life hadn't been right since the accident. Sean had been her love, her fiancé, the man she'd planned to spend her life with. When they'd had the head-on collision with the tractor-trailer rig, she'd wondered why she'd been spared and Sean had died.

Sean had been there for her when her father died. He'd been her lifeboat when she'd lost the only family she'd ever known. When he'd died instantly and she'd walked away from the accident with only bruises and cuts, she'd railed at the god that would take her only friend.

That had been the beginning of her streak of bad luck. Had she been smart, she'd have kept her distance from the brothers, insisting on a strictly boss-employee connection. Now she'd caused a rift in their apparently already rocky relationship.

Wind kicked up outside, buffeting the tin on the barn roof, finding its way through the cracks in the boards. Goose bumps rose on Lucky's arms and she nestled into the blanket, Otis snuggling up against her side.

Tired from the ranch work and then waiting tables at the Ugly Stick, Lucky let go of her worries, if only for the moment, and drifted into a deep sleep. When she woke, she'd see to the heifer, pack and be on her way to yet another fresh start. Hopefully, she'd find a place as friendly as the Ugly Stick Saloon, with people who really cared, like

Audrey, who'd take her under her wing and give her the benefit of the doubt when her luck went south. And this time, she'd be careful not to fall for one or two of the local cowboy heartbreakers.

TRENT KNOCKED on Lucky's door after a fitful night's sleep. If he could call dozing off and waking up a thousand times sleep. He'd thought a lot about how Lucky was willing to walk away rather than split up his family. The more he thought about it, the more he realized how right she was.

"Lucky." He tapped on the door. When she didn't respond, he figured she was either asleep or ignoring him. "If you're asleep, good. You worked harder than any woman I know yesterday and you deserve to sleep in. If you're not answering because you don't want to hear any more of my grumpy attitude, I'm sorry." He felt stupid talking to her door. "Please, Lucky, open the door. I need to tell you that you're right. Family is everything. I've been living alone for too long and forgot how much my brother means to me. My father and I never saw eye to eye. But Isaac always took my side when things got rough. I owe him my sanity."

Still no answer. He leaned his forehead against the door. "I won't hold it against you or Isaac if you choose him. Granted, it will be hard to see you two together, knowing I could be a part of your happiness. But I'll understand."

"You mean that?" a voice said from behind him.

Trent turned to face his brother and nodded. "I do."

"Thanks. I was getting used to having you around." Isaac smiled. "Does that mean you aren't going to sell?"

"I'm not. Even if this didn't feel like a home when I was a kid, I can make it feel like home as an adult."

"Thank goodness." Isaac draped an arm over his brother's shoulder. "I want my kids to know this place and love it like I do."

"Just be sure to encourage them to have *happy* memories."

"That's the plan." Isaac's arm dropped to his side. "What if she chooses both of us?"

Trent ran a hand through his hair, his lips twisting. "I'd be okay with that as well. It wasn't as bad as I thought it would be."

"I think it was pretty damned good." Isaac chuckled. "Is she in there?"

"I don't know. I didn't want to intrude if she was asleep."

"I'd think that if she was inside, she'd respond." Isaac gripped the doorknob and pushed it open.

The room was empty and the bed was neatly made.

Trent's heart skipped several beats. He hurried into the bedroom, threw open the closet door and nearly collapsed in relief. Lucky's duffel bag was there on the floor, her few items of clothing hanging in a tidy row. She didn't have a lot, for a woman. Most women had closets full of colorful clothing. Not Lucky. He turned back to the bedroom and noticed the worn picture frame with a faded photo on the nightstand by the bed.

He crossed to lift it.

Lucky stood beside an older, careworn man with a tanned face, cowboy hat and eyes the same color as hers. They were both smiling and happy.

His heart squeezed in his chest. This had to be Lucky's father. A man who obviously had loved his daughter.

"She deserves to be that happy again." Isaac stood beside him, staring down at the picture.

"Yes, she does."

"Question is, are we the men to make her that happy?"

Trent answered honestly, "I don't know."

"We didn't have the best example, what with Mom leaving before you were four and Dad being the horse's butt he was."

"One thing's certain," Trent said. "We know how *not* to be happy."

"She's special," Isaac noted.

"I know." Trent set the picture frame back on the nightstand. "She made me see this place."

"What do you mean?"

"Through her eyes, it's beautiful."

"I tried to tell you it wasn't the place but our father you were angry at."

Trent nodded. "That's what she showed me."

"So what are we going to do about her?" Isaac crossed his arms. "I'm willing to try and make her happy, even if it means sharing her with you."

"There's no *trying* about it. Either we make her happy or we send her on her way now and spare her the pain."

"I'm in." Isaac stuck out his hand.

Trent gripped his brother's hand and stared into his eyes. "Me too. Let's go find her and let her know."

Trent couldn't wait to see her, to hold her in his arms and dare to dream of a happier life for all of them, there at the Triple J Ranch.

They left the house and hurried toward the barn. Wind had picked up, pushing a long line of dark clouds their way.

A gust blew Isaac's cowboy hat off his head, and he ran

after it, catching it before it had gone more than a couple yards.

The vet's truck was parked outside the barn. Dr. Richards emerged, carrying his bag of medical supplies. When he saw them, he set the bag in the backseat of the four-door truck and straightened. "I dosed the heifer with antibiotics and drenched her again." He grinned. "I like the new ranch hand, she knows her stuff and could well have saved that heifer. You better keep her around. She's good."

"We know," Trent said. "Is she inside?"

"She was a few minutes ago, but left on a horse after I'd administered the antibiotics. I have to get out to the O'Briens' place before that storm hits."

"You better get going." Trent opened the door for the doctor to climb into his truck. "Thanks for coming out on short notice."

"Glad I could help. Lucky did the right thing." He nodded toward the wicked-looking sky. "You better batten down the hatches, looks like it'll be bad."

As the vet drove out of the barnyard, Trent glanced across the pasture, wondering where Lucky had gone.

Isaac checked inside the barn. Nothing moved but one of the horses in a stall. It was then he realized Thunder's stall was empty. He checked the tack room and his heart sank to his knees. Lucky had apparently taken the wildest horse out for a ride.

When he emerged from the barn, he glanced around, worried. The storm was moving in fast. Otis trotted out of the barn beside him and crossed to Trent to nuzzle his hand.

Trent brushed his fingers over the dog's short hair.

"Thunder's not in his stall and a saddle is missing from the tack room," Isaac announced.

"Surely she didn't…" Trent ran into the barn and looked for himself. When he came out, he too stared at the darkening sky. "Damn."

Isaac ran for the back of the barn and pulled the four-wheeler out, checked the gas level and shouted over the wind at his brother. "You coming?"

Trent hopped on as Isaac gunned the throttle and they were off across the pastures to find their suicidal ranch hand and the potential love of their lives.

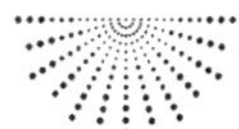

CHAPTER ELEVEN

*L*ucky gave Thunder his head, letting him race across the ground like the wind. He'd been jumpy and nervous when she'd pulled him out of his stall and saddled him up. He needed to run and she needed the wind in her hair and to get away from the house and the two men she feared she was falling for.

By the time Thunder reached the creek with the pool, they were both breathing hard and ready for a rest.

She reined in the big horse beside the clear pool and slipped from the saddle. Thunderclouds had gathered in the west and pushed up a long line of storms headed her way, which suited her mood. She'd hoped the ride would settle her thoughts, make her decisions easier and get her over the heartache building like the storm.

It hadn't. Coming to the place where she'd first experienced an orgasm with Trent didn't help. She could only imagine him here, lying naked on the rock ledge, maybe with Isaac floating in the pool. Her core heated, blood running like molten-hot liquid through her veins. The image of both of them, naked and beautiful, dappled by sunlight through the overhanging trees had her breathing hard and wishing with all her heart they were there.

But the foliage around the pool wasn't the lazy, sublime trees of the day before. The wind whipped them, making them wave like palm fronds in a hurricane.

The horse whinnied, urging her to get moving. Lightning lit up the bank of clouds followed by a low rumbling in the distance. She'd have to hurry if she wanted to get on the road before the storm hit.

Swinging up in the saddle, she gave one last glance at the pool, her chest hurting so badly she could barely breathe.

Before she could press her heels into Thunder's flanks, he bolted out of the valley and raced back toward the barn, galloping as if being chased by the storm.

When she reached the barn, Lucky hung the saddle in the tack room, rubbed the horse down, led him into the stall where she fed him sweet feed and hay and made sure he had plenty of water. "Too wild to ride, my fanny," she muttered, rubbing his nose. "Misunderstood is more the case. You just like to run."

The horse tossed his head in agreement. "If only men were as easily understood."

Thunder brushed her cheek with his nose as if sensing her melancholy.

Before leaving the barn, Lucky went to the last stall to check on the heifer. The bovine seemed to be doing better already, although she shifted nervously at the clap of thunder outside.

Done in the barn, Lucky trudged up to the house and called out, "Trent, Isaac?"

No answer.

"I'm leaving," she called again. Nothing moved inside. She went from room to room, searching for them. When she didn't find either one, she was sad and relieved at the same time. If she tried to leave with them standing there, it would be that much more difficult. Especially if they just let her go.

With tears welling in her eyes, Lucky packed her duffel bag, sliding her picture of her dad in between the clothing to keep it from breaking. Clouds obliterated the sun outside, making the room dark and gloomy.

She closed the door and walked back through the house, carrying her bag, her gaze skimming over the leather furniture in the living room and the pictures hung on the wall of horses, Texas blue bonnets and wide-open western sunsets. Though she'd only been there a short time, she'd miss this place. It was the first place she'd felt could be a home after her father died. She stopped in the kitchen for a couple pieces of bread from a loaf on the counter.

At the front door, she turned back into the house for one last look. "Goodbye," she said to no one, and then she left.

Otis met her on the porch, nuzzling the hand with the slices of bread. She let him have one, saving the other to lure him toward her truck.

Stashing her bag behind her seat, Lucky glanced around the yard and down toward the barn. Neither of the Jameson men were anywhere in sight. Lucky supposed they'd gone to town. Now would be a good time to leave the Triple J.

Then why was it still so hard?

Nobody stopped her or tried to convince her to stay. She would be on her own again, homeless and alone.

She held the passenger seat door open and tossed the other piece of bread up on the seat.

Otis jumped in.

Alone except for Otis, who happily gobbled up the piece of bread in one gulp and tried to climb into Lucky's lap when she slid behind the wheel.

"Ready to find a new home, buddy?"

Otis woofed and settled back against the seat, staring out the window as if he looked forward to the adventure.

At least someone was happy about leaving.

Lucky drove slowly out of the yard and down the long winding drive leading to the highway. Every five seconds she glanced in the rearview mirror, hoping one of the Jamesons would come riding up beside her and beg her to stay. She made it to the highway and halfway to town before she realized how idiotic she was being. They weren't coming.

But that storm was.

As she drove down Main Street in Temptation, she noted the people standing outside of the Shear Safari, staring up at the sky.

Among them was Audrey Anderson.

Lucky pulled up next to the curb and dropped down from her pickup. "Audrey, could I have a word with you?"

Audrey broke away from Mona and the woman Mona had been with the night Lucky pushed Audrey's truck into the ditch.

Audrey called back over her shoulder, "Oh, and Bunny have those flowers delivered to Charli tomorrow. It's her two-year anniversary with the Ugly Stick Saloon. I don't know what I'd do without her."

A pang of regret ripped through Lucky. She hadn't even lasted two nights, much less two years at the Ugly Stick and here she was bugging out because she was afraid of falling in love with two very handsome cowboys.

"What's up, Lucky?"

"I'm leaving."

Audrey frowned. "What do you mean, you're leaving?"

Before Lucky could respond, a shout sounded from across the street at the local attorney's office. "There she is! That's her! That's the woman who attacked me and threw me into Judge Stephen's pool." Mrs. Rutledge hurried toward her, followed by a man in a suit and another in a sheriff's deputy uniform.

Mrs. Rutledge shook her finger at Lucky. "I told you I'd sue you." She turned back to the deputy. "Serve her," she demanded.

The deputy was the same one who'd been there to take notes after the debacle in the sheriff's pool the day before. "I'm sorry, Ms. Albright. I don't always agree with these things, but I'm here to serve you with papers."

Lucky's heart dropped into the pit of her belly. "Serve me?"

"That's right. I'm taking you to court. And don't think you're going to get away with attacking people like you did in Comfort."

Audrey's brows furrowed. "What are you talking about?"

Mrs. Rutledge pointed her finger in Lucky's face. "She burned down the public library in Comfort, Texas, and practically burned the entire town down. She's bad for Temptation, I'm telling you. And I aim to have her banned from town and anywhere within a fifty-mile radius of us."

Lucky's fingers curled around the envelope the deputy handed her, her heart burning in her chest. It was happening all over again.

"You don't have to worry, Mrs. Rutledge. I'm leaving Temptation. In fact I'm leaving Texas as soon as I can get on the road."

"You are doing no such thing." Audrey stepped between Mrs. Rutledge and Lucky. "I don't know what Lucky has done in the past, but she's a good girl and an excellent waitress. I won't have you or any of your garden club witches bullying her like you bully everyone else in Temptation. If you want to bully someone, I suggest you take me on."

Mrs. Rutledge puffed out her chest and stood even taller. "I've been after the county to shut down that sorry excuse for a bar for years. With you threatening me, you've finally given me the justification to do so. Mr. Wallendorf…" she turned to the man in the business suit, "…you heard her threaten me. I want you to find a way to use that threat to shut down the Ugly Stick Saloon." She faced Audrey, eyes narrowed, a sneer curling her lip. "Mark my words, I will shut down the Ugly Stick if it's the last thing I do."

Mona and Bunny joined the crowd around Audrey and Lucky.

"You can't close the Ugly Stick Saloon. Too many people depend on it for employment."

"It's an eyesore and a place of sin," Mrs. Rutledge pronounced.

"Is not," Bunny chimed in. "It's a place where people go when they have nowhere else to go. Audrey's done more for this community and the people living here than you and your snooty garden club have."

"Alcohol consumption is a sin."

"And you being judgmental isn't?" Mona turned on

Mrs. Rutledge, placing herself between Lucky, Audrey and Mrs. Rutledge.

"Don't you get huffy with me. I have the right to tell it as it is."

"Maybe so, but that doesn't give you the right to shut down the only place cowboys and girls have to play and let their hair down after a hard week's work. We're tired of you and the Temptation Garden Club pushing people around. We're not going to take it anymore."

"You watch out or I'll have the health department shut down the Shear Safari."

Lucky groaned. Could things get any worse?

A blared siren wailed overhead, long, loud and insistent.

Everyone standing on the street around Lucky glanced up at the sky, falling silent.

"What was that?" Lucky asked.

Audrey gripped her arm. "Tornado siren."

The radio clipped to the deputy's shoulder squawked and a voice called out, "Tornado has touched down southwest of Temptation, headed northeast at sixty miles an hour. Expected to hit Temptation in less than five minutes. Seek shelter immediately."

Mona glanced around. "Come on, everybody, let's get inside."

"We need a tornado shelter," Audrey said. "We have one in the basement of the Ugly Stick, but that's too far. Where is one around here? We don't have much time."

"I don't know about shelters, but my shop used to be a bank a long time ago," Mona said. "They had a vault in the basement. The vault door was replaced with a wooden one, but the walls are concrete and it's as solid as any other tornado shelter. Come on."

"Oh, dear Lord. Dear Lord." When Mrs. Rutledge remained standing in the very spot she'd started her tirade, Mona turned back. "It's come with us or stand here and be blown away by a tornado. Your choice."

"Come on, Mrs. Rutledge, be safe. Go with Mona." Lucky motioned the woman to follow Mona. "Better safe than sorry."

The older woman glanced at the sky, the wind whipping dust into her eyes. "I can't."

Audrey gripped the woman's arm on one side. "Mrs. Rutledge, you can and will." She tried to drag her along.

The older woman's heels dug into the pavement. "I can't move." Tears streamed from her eyes and she sank to her knees, sobbing. "I can't move."

Lucky glanced at the roiling sky. They didn't have much time. Debris was flung with the wind, pelting them with dust, small sticks and tree branches. She squatted next to the sobbing woman and spoke loudly and calmly into her ear. "It's okay, Mrs. Rutledge." The judge had called her Barbara. "Barbara, I'm going to help you to your feet. Audrey and I, we'll carry you into the shelter. Hold on, you're going to be all right."

"I'm going to die," she cried.

"We won't let you." Lucky draped one of the woman's arms over her shoulders, Audrey draped the other. "On the count of three," Lucky shouted over the roaring wind.

Together, they stood, bringing Mrs. Rutledge with them. Then moving as quickly as they could with the dead-weight of the older woman between them, Lucky and Audrey got Mrs. Rutledge inside. Once behind the doors of the beauty shop, she seemed to snap out of it long enough to get herself down the steps into the basement, and thank goodness, other than pushing her down the steps, Lucky couldn't see how she or Audrey could have lifted the woman on their own.

When they were all safely in the old vault, Lucky remembered Otis, sitting in the cab of her pickup.

She ran up the steps.

"Where are you going?" Audrey shouted after her.

"My dog. I can't leave him out there." She ran through the beauty shop as heavier debris slammed into the window. A broken tree branch hit the glass, shattering it inward.

Otis, she had to get to Otis.

When she flung the shop door open, it whipped out of her hand and the wind flung her sideways. Bracing herself, she looked to the west. A wall of destruction headed straight for town, kicking up dirt from the farm fields, shattered buildings, tin roofs and more.

Lucky ran for her truck and yanked open the door.

Otis whined and refused to get out.

She reached in and dragged him to the edge. Then he leaped over her and onto the ground.

When Lucky reached for the leather collar Trent had put on him, he shot out of reach.

She followed him, buffeted by nature, the roaring increasing with each step. A branch full of leaves raked across her face and slapped her in the eyes. She blinked and refocused on Otis as he disappeared into the open doorway of a house.

"Otis!" Lucky yelled, the sound swallowed in the massive maw of the tornado bearing down on Temptation.

She dove for the door as the windows imploded, blowing glass outward.

Otis barked from the back of the house.

Lucky prayed whoever had been in the house had made

it safely to shelter. "Otis!" She ran from bedroom to bedroom. One of them was filled with children's toys, a dollhouse and pink bedspreads on the bed.

Otis's tail stuck out from beneath the bed.

Lucky grabbed his tail and yanked. "Come on, boy, we have to get somewhere safe!"

She pulled him out from under the bed, and as soon his head cleared he barked wildly.

"I know. I'm scared too."

When she tried to drag him back through the house, he yanked free and ran back into the bedroom where he barked at the bed.

Dread washed over Lucky as she ran after Otis. Dropping to her knees, she peered beneath the bed and spied a small girl and a little boy crouched beneath. Tears streaked down their faces.

"Oh my God." Lucky reached out to the children. "Come with me. We have to get to safety. Please!"

The little boy crawled out. He had to be about six, and he was shaking and scared.

When the girl wouldn't come, Lucky lay down on her belly and grabbed the girl's ankle and dragged her out. She grabbed both of them up in her arms and ran for the bathroom, tossed them into the tub and ran back to the bedroom for a mattress to throw over them. A glance out the window showed a greenish-black sky, and flying debris made up of two-by-fours, siding, insulation and more. The town was being ripped apart.

A figure lay on the ground outside in the backyard, a woman, possibly the children's mother.

Lucky ran back to the bathroom threw the mattress on top of the kids and raced out the back door.

The wind lifted her up and slammed her back against

the house. She fought her way forward, her arm over her eyes, protecting her vision from sharp objects.

When she reached the woman, she grabbed her arm and dragged her toward the house. "Get up!" she yelled.

The woman moaned, the sound barely audible over the screaming wail of the wind.

The mother staggered to her feet and, with Lucky's help, made it into the house and the bathroom as the full force of the tornado descended on Temptation, hitting it hard.

Huddled beneath the mattress, two frightened children and their mother crying beside her, Lucky prayed Trent and Isaac were okay.

She made a promise to herself that if she made it through the storm, she'd go back to the Triple J Ranch. No more running. No more feeling sorry for herself. She'd stand up to that crappy streak of bad luck and tackle it head-on. And she'd go after the two men she had grown to admire in the short time she'd known them and see what happened. If they wanted her to stick around, she would. If they didn't, she'd be okay too. Sad, but okay.

She wanted to shake her fist at the tornado, to rail against the destruction and to shout, *The bad luck ends here*!

CHAPTER TWELVE

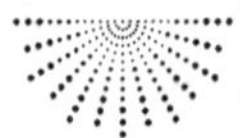

Trent crushed the accelerator to the floorboard. The truck flew down the highway straight for Temptation and right into the eye of the storm.

"Holy hell," Isaac muttered beside him.

Rocks, sticks, nails, pieces from farm implements pummeled the truck in the back draft from what looked like an F5 tornado as it steamrolled over the little town of Temptation, demolishing everything in its path.

They'd driven the four-wheeler over the property, trying to guess where Lucky would have gone riding. After twenty minutes, they'd given up, the sky getting so dark they reasoned she had to have headed back to the barn.

When Isaac parked the ATV outside the barn, Trent ran in and found Thunder in his stall, the saddle back in its place in the tack room.

He ran out of the barn and up to the house, glancing back over his shoulder at the wall of clouds with little wisps dropping down from beneath it. Funnel clouds.

His pulse pounding, he burst through the back door and ran for Lucky's bedroom. "Lucky!"

She wasn't there, the picture that had been on her nightstand was gone and so were the clothes and duffel bag she'd had in her closet.

"Her truck is gone!" Isaac yelled from down the hall. "Lucky's gone."

Trent pushed past him, grabbed his keys from the counter in the kitchen and headed out the front door.

"Where are you going?" Isaac shouted over the wind.

"*We* are going after her." He hopped into the driver's seat of his pickup. "Get in."

Isaac barely sat in his seat when Trent floored the accelerator and shot out of the yard.

Now they were racing into a storm that appeared to have swallowed the entire town they'd grown up in.

His heart heavy, his heart pounding against his ribs, Trent didn't let up on the gas. People he knew and loved were there. He hoped they'd made it to shelter. He prayed they'd live to rebuild.

"Fuck, look at it." Isaac stared through the windshield. "It must be a mile wide at its base."

"All those people," Trent said.

"And Lucky. I hope she went the other direction."

Trent prayed for the same. His gut told him the opposite.

By the time they reached the edge of town, the tornado had moved on, leaving in its wake a horrifying swath of destruction.

From what Trent could tell, it had come in from the west, plowed through town, leveling homes, businesses and everything in its path.

Trent pulled the truck to the side of the road and parked. He reached beneath his seat and unearthed a couple pair of work gloves, handing a set to Isaac. "We can't go any farther by vehicle. We have to walk from here."

They dropped down and picked through the rubble, working their way through what had once been Main Street.

Many of the buildings were gone. The ones still standing had entire walls ripped away, or roofs lifted and thrown across the street.

People slowly began to emerge, crawling out from beneath the rubble, cut, scraped and dazed.

"Help!" a woman yelled. "Help us! We're in here." More voices called out from below a pile of wood, insulation and glass.

Trent and Isaac pulled away broken beams, dry wall and roof shingles. Beneath that they found broken porcelain shampoo bowls and vinyl-covered adjustable chairs.

"This must be the Shear Safari," Isaac said.

"Mona? Are you in there?" Trent called out.

"We're down here, in the basement."

"How many?"

"Six of us," Mona answered.

"Is Lucky with you?" Isaac threw boards and beauty shop equipment to the side.

"No, she went back for that dog."

Trent dug faster, careful with the glass and electrical lines. If Lucky wasn't with them, where had she gone?

After twenty minutes of steady work, they found the door, cleared a path and helped Mona, Bunny, Audrey, Mrs. Rutledge, Deputy Cramer and Mr. Wallendorf, one of the four attorneys in town. With nothing more than scratches, bruises and a layer of dust, they appeared to be fine, if a little dazed.

"You say Lucky was here before it hit?" Trent asked Mona.

"She helped me get Mrs. Rutledge into the basement," Audrey responded. "Then she ran out, saying something about a dog."

Trent glanced at his brother and they both said, "Otis" at the same time.

Back out on the pavement, they looked around. More people were crawling out from beneath what was left of houses and businesses.

A vehicle lay on its side, pushed up against the trunk of a tree, the top of which had been snapped off like a broken twig.

Trent and Isaac rounded the vehicle and stopped. "It's her truck."

Lucky hadn't made it out of town. Which meant she was still somewhere in all the mess.

Trent stared around at the disaster, wondering where to start in their search when he heard a dog's bark.

He and Isaac turned toward the sound.

"You thinking what I'm thinking?" Isaac asked. Without waiting for a response, he picked his way across the rubble.

Another bark led them directly to the flattened remains of what had once been a small cottage a block off Main Street.

As they neared, the barking grew louder, sounding as if it emanated from beneath an eight-foot section of collapsed wall.

Trent positioned himself on one end of the wall while Isaac positioned himself on the other.

"On the count of three," Trent said. "One, two, three!" He put all his strength into it and the wall wouldn't budge.

The dog barked again and again, growing more frantic with each bark.

Jackson, Mark and Luke Gray Wolf hurried across the debris toward them and threw their backs into moving the wall.

With the help of all five men, they lifted and shoved the wall over, clearing what looked like a small bathroom. A mattress lay over what had once been the tub.

Almost afraid to look beneath, Trent grabbed one end of the mattress, while Mark Gray Wolf hefted the other and they threw it to the side.

As they cleared the mattress, Otis leaped out of a bathtub and landed beside Trent, jumping up on him, trying to lick his face.

Trent pushed him down and looked into the tub.

A woman lay across the length of the tub, her body covering something beneath.

Little arms and legs moved beneath the body and a child cried out.

Trent moved the body, lifting it up and away from two children and a woman lying beneath. The limp body he'd pealed back was Lucky.

"Lucky." Isaac lifted her into his arms and carried her over to a spot on the ground Luke cleared enough to lay her down. Trent knelt beside her and felt for her pulse. After a long moment, he let go of the breath he'd been holding and almost collapsed over Lucky. "She's alive."

Mark and Luke lifted the children out and held them crying in their arms.

The people who'd been trapped in the beauty salon made their way toward them. Mrs. Rutledge crying out when Jackson pulled the woman out of the tub. "Oh, dear

Lord, Nan!" She rushed forward and dropped to the ground where Jackson laid the woman.

Nan's eyes blinked open. "Aaron and Emma?" she asked.

"Mommy?" the little boy called out, reaching for his mother. Mark held him back, dropping to a squat so the mother and child could see each other. Luke lowered the little girl as well.

"Oh, babies. I'm so glad you're okay." Nan reached out to cup each child's face. "Thank God for our angel of mercy," she said. "We were lucky she came along when she did."

"What are you talking about?" Mrs. Rutledge asked.

"The woman who saved us." Nan closed her eyes. "I must have been hit by some debris, 'cause the next thing I knew, a woman came out of nowhere, dragged me into the house and into the tub where Aaron and Emma were. She saved our lives."

Mrs. Rutledge glanced over at the still form of Lucky, lying as pale as a ghost against the ground. "Lucky did that?" she asked.

Trent stared down at Lucky. "Sounds like something she'd do."

"Is she…is she going to live?" Mrs. Rutledge asked, her eyes rounded, filling with tears. "I owe her for saving my daughter and grandchildren."

"I hope so." Trent straightened and looked around. "We have to get her to the hospital."

"If it's still standing."

The deputy joined them. "Thank God it missed the hospital. The road crews are clearing a path so that the ambulance can get in here. We have other units coming in from Hole in the Wall that should be here in less than fifteen minutes and more help is on its way from all over the state."

Lucky moaned.

Trent dropped down beside her, Isaac on the other side.

Her eyes blinked open and she stared up at them. "The kids?"

"They're okay, thanks to you," Isaac said.

"Mom?"

"Alive and okay." Trent tucked a strand of her hair behind her ear. "Again, thanks to you." He bent to kiss her forehead.

"That would feel a whole lot better on my booboos," she whispered.

"Just tell us where they are and we'll take care of all of them," Isaac said.

Lucky chuckled and winced. "Ouch." Then she raised her hand pointing to her cheek where a dark bruise was just beginning to show. "There."

Trent bent to press a feather-soft kiss to the spot.

She raised her other arm and pointed to a spot on the side of her chin. "There."

Isaac laughed and kissed her there, careful not to hurt her.

Then she touched her finger to her lips and peeked through lowered eyelids. "There."

Trent bent at the same time as Isaac and their heads collided. He backed up and motioned for his brother. "You first."

Isaac claimed her lips in a gentle kiss. When he came up, he said. "One is not enough."

"Tell me about it," she whispered, her gaze going to Trent.

He leaned over her and kissed her, his tongue pushing

through to slide along hers. Despite nearly being killed, maybe because she'd nearly died, she tasted like heaven.

No, it was because she was Lucky.

"Hey, let her breathe."

Isaac's hand on his shoulder made him pull back. "I'm sorry."

Lucky lay with her eyes closed, the corners of her lips turned up. "Didn't hear me complainin', did you?"

Trent laughed. "Lucky Albright, I'm convinced."

"About what, cowboy?"

"That the day you showed up at the Ugly Stick Saloon was the luckiest day of my life." Trent kissed her on the lips again, in a brief, happy kiss.

"And mine," Isaac agreed. "We had been talking about you before you even showed up."

"You did?" Her eyes opened, a small frown denting her forehead. "How's that?"

Jackson laughed. "Trent and Isaac were listing the qualities they expected in the perfect woman."

"And there you were," Isaac said.

Lucky's mouth twisted. "Wrecking Audrey's truck and her storeroom of liquor."

Audrey laughed softly, slipping into Jackson's arms. "All of that can be replaced." She smiled down at Lucky. "Can I safely say that my new employee will be back on the job as soon as she's feeling up to it?"

Lucky glanced up at Trent and Isaac. "I don't know."

"If you're asking if she's staying," Trent said, "the answer is yes."

"Damn right she is." Isaac brought her hand to his lips. "We kind of like having her around and think she'll be around as long as she can stand the two of us."

Audrey's eyes lit up. "So that's how it is? Well then, congratulations."

Trent smiled at Isaac and held out his hand. "To partnerships."

Isaac grinned. "To not selling our home."

Lucky placed her hand over their combined hands. "How about to making it a home?"

"Agreed," both Trent and Isaac said at once.

Lucky tried to sit up.

Trent laid a hand on her shoulder. "Not yet. Let the medics take care of you. We need you in top shape when you come back."

"So that I can shovel horse manure and build fences."

"Of course," Trent said, giving her a teasing look. "No, really, you're going to have all you can handle keeping up with the two of us."

Lucky lay back, smiling. "I'll be up for the challenge. Will you two be?"

"Trent, Isaac! Where are you?" Lucky entered the house after her trip to town. "Mona sends her love. We need to hurry or we'll be late for the party fundraiser at the Ugly Stick Saloon. Audrey got us front-row seats for the concert."

FEMA had set up shop on the outskirts of Temptation, bringing with it help for those who'd lost their homes and businesses.

Mona had rented a portable building for her beauty shop while hers was being rebuilt and Bunny had a matching portable right next to hers.

Slowly but surely the resilient people of Temptation had come together and were rebuilding.

Lucky was proud to be one of them.

"I saw Barbara, Nan, Aaron and Emma at the store. They all told me to say hello. They want you to come to the next garden club meeting."

She checked in the living room, the kitchen and was heading down the hallway when she heard sounds from the bedroom.

A guarded *shh* sound came from behind the master bedroom door.

Lucky grinned. She loved sharing a bedroom with the two of them, the king-sized bed perfect for them to sleep or whatever they wanted to do in it.

The whatever was the fun part and thoughts of all the possibilities had her body heating. She toed off her boots and set them to the side of the door.

By the time she shimmied out of her jeans, she was fully turned on and ready for the two of them. She yanked her shirt over her head and tossed it to the floor. Wearing nothing but her bra and panties, she twisted the doorknob. "Ready or not, here I come." Thrusting the door open she stepped inside, her bare feet tickled by rose petals spread all over the floor.

"What's this?" She stared around the room. The curtains had been drawn, making the room dark. Candles had been lit all around, the scent of sandalwood filling the air and, down the center of the mattress was a layer of the red rose petals. The best part was that both men stood naked on either side of the king-sized bed.

"What's the occasion?" she said, loving the feel of the petals against her feet.

Isaac smiled. "Our two-month anniversary since you came to live with us."

"You're over dressed for the occasion. It's clothing restricted," Trent said.

"The rose petals were my idea," Isaac said.

"Naked was mine." Trent shifted and growled. "And you know how much I don't much like being naked with only another man in the room. Are you coming or do I have to come get you?"

"Oh, I'll be coming soon enough," she said, crawling

onto the center of the bed. "Although I could use a little help with the clasp on the back of my bra." Rising to her knees, she turned her back to Isaac who made quick work of the hooks and slipped the bra over her shoulders.

Trent climbed onto the bed, flipped her onto her back and dragged her panties down her legs, tossing them to the corner. Then he spread her knees wide and lay down between them, his tongue tracing the inside of her thigh to her center. "Better. Much better."

"I'll say." Isaac claimed a breast, flicking his tongue across her nipple as it tightened into a hard bead. He scooped a handful of petals from the bed and dropped them over her breasts and belly. "Did you like the roses?"

With Trent's tongue swirling around her entrance, she answered, "Yes!"

"Bunny helped me with them."

"Remind me to thank her." Trent swiped his tongue across her clit and she arched her back, her heels digging into the mattress. "Oh, there. Please, there."

Trent chuckled and settled in to bring her to the edge. Just the way she liked it.

As Isaac sucked her breast into his mouth, she wrapped her hand around his cock and squeezed gently. "I want *you* inside me first," she said. With her other hand, she brushed through Trent's hair. "And, Trent, honey, I want to taste your cock."

Trent flopped onto his back, his legs dangling off the bed.

Lucky rolled off the bed, bent to take Trent's dick between her lips and sucked hard, pulling him deep into her mouth.

Isaac grabbed her hips, cupped her sex with one hand and ran his finger around her slick opening.

Anxious to feel him inside her, Lucky pulled her mouth free of Trent and urged, "Fuck me now, cowboy."

As Isaac thrust into her from behind, he sprinkled rose petals over her ass.

Lucky slid her lips down over Trent.

With her mouth full of one cowboy and her pussy full of another, she didn't think life could get much better.

Isaac thrust into her again and again, until he thrust one last time, held her steady and tight against him, his cock pulsing inside her.

Trent pumped in and out of her mouth, his body becoming more rigid with each thrust. Finally, he pulled free of Lucky's lips.

His face strained, Trent dragged Lucky onto the mattress, her legs dangling over the side, the scent of roses, filling her senses. In one slow, easy thrust, he entered her.

Isaac lay down beside her and stroked her breast, pinching the tip until it knotted into a tight little bead.

Lucky loved it when these men made love to her. They were strong, sexy and loving in the way they treated her with care and respect, and the way they played out all her sexual fantasies.

"Life does not get better than this," she said, breathless and nearly there.

"Sounds like a challenge to me." Isaac's fingers drifted down over her belly to her clit, where he stroked her while Trent pounded into her hard and fast, the way he liked it. By the time he came, it only took a couple more flicks and her nerves exploded, sending her rocketing to the heavens.

"Correction," she said. "It *does* get better."

If you enjoyed this book, try the other books in the

Ugly Stick Saloon Series

Boots & Chaps (#1)
Boots & Sex Ed (#2)
Boots & Leather (#3)
Boots & Promises (#4)
Boots & Bareback (#5)
Boots & Dirty Tricks (#6)
Boots & Lace (#7)
Boots & Roses (#8)
Boots & Buckles (#9)
Boots & the Wishes (#10)
Boots & Twisters (#11)
Boots & the Bachelor (#12)
Boots & The Rogue (#13)
Boots & The Heartbreaker (#14)
Boots & Wings (#15)

BOOTS & THE BACHELOR

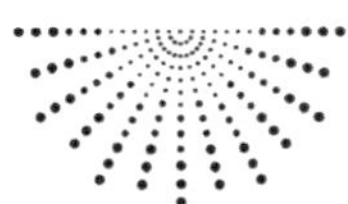

UGLY STICK SALOON SERIES BOOK #12

by
New York Times Bestselling Author
Elle James

writing as

Myla Jackson

BOOTS
& the
BACHELOR
UGLY STICK SALOON
New York Times Bestselling Author
ELLE JAMES
writing as
MYLA JACKSON

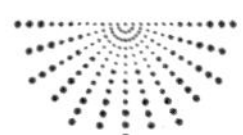

"You going to do *what?*" Angus McFarlan slammed his palm on the dining table, too angry to finish the fried chicken, mashed potatoes and gravy his mother had prepared for their dinner.

Maggie, Angus's mother and the matriarch of the McFarlan family, sat at the head of the table where John McFarlan used to sit. She folded her arms. "You heard me. I'm selling the ranch."

Her words hit him again like a sucker punch to the gut.

"Mom, you can't be serious!" Colin, the youngest of the McFarlan brothers, pushed back his chair so fast it fell with a loud crash. "You can't sell the Rafter M Ranch. It's been in the family for over one hundred and fifty years. It's our legacy. Dad would roll over in his grave."

Their mother gave an unladylike snort and tilted her chin. "I don't see any of my sons giving enough of a damn to see that legacy passed down. And your father would not want me or any of you saddled with it until your dying day only for it to be auctioned off anyway."

Angus sucked in a deep breath and let it out slowly, trying to calm himself before he shouted. His mother's declaration had thrown him for a loop, but it didn't excuse him from disrespecting her. Taking the mature, calm tact, he said in a softer tone, "Don't I work my ass off on this ranch to make it pay? When cattle prices dropped, wasn't I able to redirect our ranching efforts to keep the ranch paying for itself?"

"Angus has put his heart and soul into this place." Colin waved his hand. "He even put his climb up the corporate ladder on hold to take over when Dad died. If he hadn't ramped up the horse breeding and training, we'd have lost the ranch years ago."

"You're only making me more determined. This ranch isn't just a legacy, it's an albatross."

Angus stared at his mother, wondering where was the woman who'd always been optimistic, loving and as hard working as any of her sons? "I don't understand. The ranch is paying for itself and has been making a profit over the last three years. Why sell?"

She pointed a finger at Colin. "For the very reason you say we should keep it."

Colin's eyes widened and then narrowed into a frown. "What reason? You're not making sense, Mom."

"This ranch is a legacy. But what good is a legacy if you don't have anyone to pass it down to?" She folded her napkin and laid it beside her plate of uneaten chicken. "Angus, you and Colin work this ranch, and you work your other jobs as well. Which leaves you exactly how much time off to date, find a nice girl and settle down?" Planting her hands on the table, she stared from one to the other of her sons. "I'll tell you. No time, whatsoever. You can't get a life when you're too busy making a living on this ball and chain of a ranch." She pushed away from the table and stood. "I'm selling the ranch."

Angus stood when his mother did, his thoughts tumbling in his head. "You can't mean it, Mom. This ranch is the McFarlan home."

"Ha!" His mother stamped her foot. "If it's the McFarlan home, why hasn't Brody been back in eight years?"

Colin's lips thinned. "Ask Brody."

Angus shook his head. He wasn't sure why Brody left home eight years ago, but it had something to do with a fight he had with Colin. Colin had never owned up to what started it. "He came for your birthday last year," Angus pointed out.

Again, his mother snorted. "For an entire day. That's it. He doesn't consider this home, and he never stays."

"So? Brody doesn't consider this home, but Angus and I do," Colin said.

Angus changed tactics and tried a little reverse psychology. "Mom, this ranch is yours. Dad left it to you, and you have the right to sell it, if that's what you want."

Colin gasped. "What the hell are you saying, Angus?"

Angus held up his hand. "Dad left the ranch to Mom. It's hers, not ours."

"You and I both have put our blood and sweat into making this place sustainable," Colin said. "Doesn't that count for anything?"

"Not when the deed is in my name." Their mother stood with her chin tipped upward, her eyes narrowed. "Look, I appreciate that you both came home after your father died and stayed through my surgery and chemotherapy when I had breast cancer, but now it's time for you two to get a life and quit worrying about me or the ranch."

"Mom," Angus said. "We would have left, if we had

wanted to, but we don't. We love this place as much as Dad did."

"It's not enough." She raised her hands. "I want my boys married, with kids of their own. As I see it, this ranch is standing in the way of that ever happening. Therefore, I'm selling the ranch."

"So you're serious about the legacy thing?" Angus laughed. "Has Mrs. Reinhardt been bragging about her grandbabies again?"

"No, it's not that." She stopped, chewed on her bottom lip and tilted her head. "Well, a little. Seeing pictures of Jean's grandchildren only brought it home to me that my boys aren't moving on with their lives."

"We're happy with the way we are, Mom." Angus took his mother's hands in his. "Can't you be happy for us?"

She pulled her hands free of his and planted them on her hips. "Angus McFarlan, you're not happy and you don't even know it."

Colin stared up at the ceiling and then back at his mother. "Look at the statistics. Less than fifty percent of marriages last these days."

"Colin has a point," Angus agreed. "Why bother getting married when numbers are against you?"

"Ha!" His mother stamped her foot. "When everyone told you that you couldn't make money training horses, you didn't let that stop you, did you, Angus? I did the research and the *numbers* were against you. But you did it anyway and you made it work. And how did you do that?"

"You know I love horses, and I worked my butt off to make it work."

"Exactly," she said. "And relationships are the same. If you love someone, you have to work hard to make the marriage work. Your father and I fought, didn't we?"

Colin chuckled. "You both gave as good as you got."

"And we never went to bed mad at each other. It took a lot of compromise and work to make our relationship last. Just like with anything worthwhile in life." She nodded toward Colin. "When you started your construction business, you hardly had two nickels to rub together. You worked on building relationships with your subcontractors and with the community. That wasn't easy, was it?"

"No, but that's different."

"No, it's not." Maggie McFarlan shook her head. "You have to feed and nurture a relationship, whether it's business or personal. They don't just happen."

Angus hadn't met a woman worth all the fuss. "Frankly, Mom, I prefer talking to horses than to women. They don't talk back, and they aren't a lot of drama."

His mother's brows shot up. "Dexter, your quarter horse stud, doesn't cause a lot of drama?"

Angus's lips curled upward. "Dexter is special."

His mother rolled her eyes. "And you put up with his tantrums, the many times he breaks through fences or terrorizes the geldings and everything else, because he's *special?*" Her chest rose and fell on a long breath. "A woman can be special too, and worth the effort."

"Dexter generates a lot of money through his stud services," Angus said, hating that he sounded defensive.

Maggie stamped her foot. "Damn it, Angus, there's more to life than money."

"Mom, mom, mom." Colin, ever the charmer, slipped his arm around their mother's shoulders. "You're just upset. Mrs. Reinhardt brags about everything. It's not worth getting your shorts in a twist."

Angus stepped back as the color rose in his mother's cheeks and fire blazed in her eyes. He knew better than to patronize his mother. Colin's usual soothing tactics weren't going to work on her this time. In fact, they appeared to be about to backfire.

Bracing himself, Angus waited for his sweet, kind, rarely angry mother to erupt like a volcano.

She lifted Colin's arm and stepped out from beneath it. "My decision stands. I'm selling the ranch, unless you three McFarlan boys prove to me this ranch is a legacy that *will* have someone to pass on to."

Angus's back straightened, his body stiff. "Smells like an ultimatum to me."

"I don't care if it smells like cow paddies." Angus's mother's fist clenched. "You three boys better get it together and find wives, settle down and have some kids, or this place is gone."

"Three?" Colin frowned. "Brody doesn't even live here."

"Then you better find a way to get him back. I won't go through the rest of my days with one son running away from home for the rest of his life." She spun and marched out of the kitchen.

"She's just pulling our chain, right?" Colin rubbed his chin, staring at the empty doorway.

Angus cringed. Colin had spoken all too soon. Their mother had excellent hearing from clear across the house. Three…two…one…

Their mother reappeared in the doorway. "Here's pulling your chain: I have a real estate broker coming tomorrow to discuss breaking up and selling this ranch, however it has to be done. I'll give you boys one month to fix what's broke between Colin and Brody, get Brody back and get married. If you can't do that in one month, I'm listing this place and entertaining all offers."

"One month!" Angus thundered. "How can you expect us to meet and marry a woman in one month? It's insane."

"Okay, I'll give you two. But no more. And it's all or none. This deal includes your brother Brody."

"But—" Colin started.

Their mother held up her hand. "It's not up for negotiation." She spun, took one step and spun back. "Oh, and just to make it clear, I'm done cooking, cleaning and running your errands. If you want clean laundry or a cooked meal, do it yourself. I've made it far too easy on you boys. It's time you grew up, and, for that matter, it's time I got a life of my own."

Angus crossed his arms. "And where are we supposed to meet these women you want us to marry? Most of the ones I know are married or taken."

His mother smiled. "You boys are in luck. It's ladies' night at the Ugly Stick Saloon. There will be a whole herd of women. It's a good start and a good way to prove you're taking me seriously. I suggest you both shower, put on your best boots and get over there."

"You can't threaten us to get married," Colin grumbled.

Their mother's eyes narrowed. "No, but I can sell the ranch. And I will."

"I HAVEN'T BEEN to the Ugly Stick Saloon in seven years." Gwendolyn Graves glanced around the bar's interior crammed full of women. "I guarantee I've never seen it this packed."

Mona Daley laughed. "This is the Annual Cowboy Auction. The event brings in women from all over the state, and even Oklahoma and Arkansas. The money raised is always for a good cause and we have a ball. You remember Bunny Leigh, don't you?"

"I do." Gwen smiled. "She loved arranging flowers. How is she doing? If I remember correctly, she was just getting married."

Mona's lips curved upward. "The good news is that she owns her own flower shop now." She frowned. "The bad news is that marriage didn't last. But then it's good news." Mona waved her hand. "Sounds confusing, but she ditched the cheating bastard, bought herself two handsome cowboys at one of these cowboy auctions, and is now living happily with both of them."

Gwendolyn blinked. "My goodness. I don't know whether to offer her my condolences or congratulations."

"Congratulations. She's never been more sexually satisfied."

Nodding, Gwen said, "Wow. Two cowboys?"

"Two of the hottest cowboys in the tricounty area. And she's over-the-moon happy."

"Are *they* happy?" Gwen's core tightened at the thought of having two men to satisfy her every sexual desire. Hell, she'd be happy to have just one.

"The guys have always been really close. Sharing Bunny came natural. What about you?" Mona waved her mug of beer at Gwendolyn. "Have you finally started dating? We have to do a better job of keeping in touch. It's not like you're halfway around the world. You're only in Dallas. Once a year get-togethers aren't nearly enough."

"I know." Gwen tucked a stray strand of hair behind her ear. "You knew I took over as CEO of the small cosmetics company I worked for, didn't you?"

"Honey, you didn't just take over as CEO, you bought

the damned company." Mona leaned over and hugged her. "I read about it in the newspaper. Congratulations."

Her cheeks warmed. "Thank you. But owning your own company is very time-consuming. Especially when you're trying to expand and grow it as much as I have. I haven't had time to breathe for the past year. I've gone from ten employees to over forty."

Mona whistled. "I don't know how you do it. I can barely manage my shop and I'm the only one working there."

Gwen laid a hand on her friend's arm. "Honey, small can be so much easier. I don't have time for anything but work."

"What about your love life?"

With a snort, Gwen shook her head. "No time." And, sadly, no desire.

"That summer you came home from college, I thought for sure you and Angus McFarlan were a thing." Mona tilted her head. "What happened with that?"

"I went back to college." Gwen shrugged. "He never contacted me."

"That's too bad. You two seemed perfect together."

She'd thought so too. On their last date, he'd taken her to the top of a hill on the Rafter M Ranch in his pickup. They'd stretched out a blanket on the grass, made love beneath a star-studded Texas sky and fallen asleep in each other's arms. In the middle of the night, she'd woken beside him, so filled with love and longing. The last thing she wanted to do was return to College Station to finish her degree.

Had he asked her to marry him that night, she'd have said yes and chucked college.

But he hadn't. Angus had told her how important it was

for her to get her education, and that he understood she had to leave. Feeling optimistic that he'd wait for her, she'd tucked a letter in the back pocket of his jeans, telling him the things she'd been too shy to say out loud. She loved him and hoped he'd wait for her. At the bottom, she'd given him her phone number and address in College Station and told him to call her if he got the chance.

Two months passed and he didn't write, call or visit. At Christmas when she would normally have gone home for the holidays, her parents announced they'd sold the house, bought a motor home and would be spending the winter in Florida.

Angus hadn't contacted her by Christmas and, with no family left in Temptation, she had no reason to return.

"How's Dalton doing in his new school?" Mona's question pulled her back to the present. "What is he, six now?"

"He'll be six soon." Her son was the center of Gwen's world. A child born out of stupid sex and a quickie marriage in Vegas, Dalton was the farthest thing from a mistake. He was her everything. "Dalton is the perfect son. He's respectful, loving, kind to animals and smart as a whip."

Mona clapped her hands. "And I bet Grant is having a ball as we speak. You should have seen him going through his old sports stuff from his high school days when I told him you were coming."

"I didn't come down from Dallas to stick Grant with babysitting." Gwen sighed. "I needed a break from work and the city, and it's been far too long since I came to visit you here in Temptation."

"Damn right it has. Seven years to be exact. Hell, since your parents sold out and moved to Florida."

"I miss this place."

"I miss you." Mona set her beer mug on the bar and hugged her friend. "I'm glad I talked you into girls' night out."

"I am too. It's been a while since I've had a night out. Much as I love my son, it's nice to have a break."

Mona settled back on her barstool and drank a swallow of beer. "So you traveled all the way to Temptation just to see me?"

"I needed to talk to someone who wasn't from the city. Someone down-to-earth."

Mona's brows crinkled. "That doesn't sound sexy at all. You're making me feel like my grandmother."

Gwen laughed. "Not at all. You're young, vibrant and…" her lips twisted as she thought how to phrase her words, "…well, everything I feel like I've lost in myself."

"What?" Mona leaned back. "Look at you. You're a freakin' knockout. I can't even offer to do your hair. You must have some high-dollar stylist at your beck and call."

Heat rushed up in her cheeks. "Yeah. I do. But that's not why I came. I need advice."

"You're the owner of a growing company. What would I know about the world you don't know already?"

"I have Dalton in a good school. They wear uniforms every day and they have high academic standards. He's almost six, but he's reading at a fourth-grade level already."

"And that's a problem?" Mona's brow scrunched. "I don't see a problem."

"I'm a single mom, raising a son. I teach him right from wrong, to be kind to others and help him with his home-work. I'm doing the best I can." Gwen twisted her hands together.

Mona smiled across her beer. "What child needs more than that?"

"*He* does. He's a good kid, but I can't be everything to him." Gwen sighed. "He needs a male role model. One he can look up to. A man who can teach him what it takes to be a good man."

Mona nodded. "You're smart, what is it you can't do that a man could?"

Gwen raised a finger. "For one, I can't throw a baseball to save my life. I'm even worse at football. I admit, I'm hopeless when it comes to sports."

"So?" Mona laughed. "Sign him up for a community team. I'm sure Dallas has loads of them."

"They do, but it's not just that." Gwen raised a second finger. "He needs to know how to defend himself."

"Put him in a martial arts class."

"I could do that, but it's more than classes and sports. He needs a role model, someone he can talk to and ask guy questions."

Mona gave her a pointed look. "Then why aren't you dating? If you found a man you could love, he could provide Dalton with that male role model you think he needs."

"That's like interviewing men for a position as my son's father." Gwen grimaced. "I wouldn't do that to the man, and I wouldn't want to marry a man I don't love just to give Dalton a dad."

"Give yourself a break, sweetie. You might find the perfect guy you and Dalton could both love."

Gwen shook her head. "It's too much to ask a guy to take on a ready-made family. I've given up on marriage and dating until Dalton is grown and on his own."

"Wow, that's harsh."

"It's reality. Besides, I don't have time for a man in my life."

"I think you protest too much." Mona grinned. "When was the last time you got laid?"

Gwen gasped. "Mona!"

Her friend shrugged. "A woman has needs, just like a man."

"We were talking about my son. Not me."

"Fine. Have it your way." Mona chugged the last of her beer and set it on the counter. "But I think you need a man to give you some hot, dirty sex to get your female juices flowing again. Your vagina is like any other muscle. It needs to be exercised or it shrivels up from lack of use."

Gwen clapped both hands to her burning cheeks. "Mona, please. Change the subject. You're embarrassing me." And making her hot just thinking about exercising her woman parts. God, it had been far too long since she'd had a man in her bed and her vibrator just wasn't getting her off anymore.

Mona pushed her mug toward Libby, the bartender. "Can you set us up with a couple of tequila shots?"

Libby plopped two shot glasses on the counter and spilled tequila into them, then she sliced a lime into quarters and set them in a glass beside the tequila shots. "Want salt with that?"

"Damn right," Mona said.

Libby plunked a shaker of salt beside the tequila and limes. "Let me know when you need a refill."

Mona lifted a shot glass. "You remember how, right? It's as easy as one, two, three. Salt." She licked the curve in her hand between her thumb and forefinger, shook salt over where she'd licked and then sucked the salt off her hand. "Tequila." Mona upended her shot glass, downing the tequila in one swallow. "Lime." Jamming the lime in her mouth, she bit into the fruit, her face puckering. "Whew!

That burns so good." She nodded toward the other shot glass. "Your turn."

Gwen hadn't done tequila shots since college and stared at the shot glass skeptically. Then she shrugged and performed the same routine—salt, tequila, lime—downing the liquid in one fiery gulp.

The alcohol burned down her throat all the way to her stomach, shooting flames outward to her extremities.

After a moment, the alcohol settled in, numbing the back of her throat first, then her tongue and finally the tips of her fingers.

"Have you thought about getting Dalton into a mentoring program?"

"No, I hadn't thought about that," she said, her tongue feeling heavy and a bit slow. "How would I know I'd be getting a good one?"

"You could screen them." Mona glanced around the saloon at the laughing, giggling women. "Hell, Gwen, buy a cowboy tonight. Audrey only invites the best to be auctioned. They have to be polite, with no criminal record, and an all-around good guy, or she wouldn't let them be auctioned off."

Heat filled Gwen's cheeks. "I couldn't do that. These men are expecting to go on a date with a *woman*. Not a woman and her son."

"I bet they wouldn't mind. That would give you a jump start with that male role model you want. He might even teach Dalton how to ride."

The thought held merit. Dalton had been pestering her for riding lessons. Who better to teach him than a cowboy? She could arrange to have the dates at a local riding stable. Dalton and the cowboy could ride while she watched from the other side of the fence.

"And you might find that you like the cowboy, fall in love and the three of you will live happily ever after." Mona hopped off her stool. "I'll be right back."

"Where are you going?" Gwendolyn had met Audrey Anderson, the owner, and Libby, the bartender, but she didn't know anyone else in the crowded room.

Mona waved a hand as she disappeared into the crowd.

"Can I get you another drink?" Libby asked.

Gwen stared down at the empty shot glass, warmth still floating through her, and smiled. "Yes, please." Seven summers ago, Angus had taught her an appreciation for tequila right there in the Ugly Stick Saloon. She glanced around, half hoping to see the man who'd ruined her for any other man. He'd set the bar too high for any of the men she'd dated, and they never quite rose to that level.

Angus was kindhearted, loved his family, kept his promises, and he was good with animals. Not to mention, he was an excellent lover. Her thighs tingled. She tried to count it off as the tequila still working its way through her system, but she knew that would be a lie.

The memories of Angus lying between her legs, making sweet love to her in the bed of his pickup, on the sweet-scented prairie grass and in the secluded hunter's cabin on a far corner of the Rafter M Ranch, were never far from her mind.

He was the kind of man she wanted as a role model for her son. A man's man, who knew how to treat a woman. Then again, he'd failed in one category. He'd never come after her.

She'd learned a valuable lesson with Angus McFarlan. Don't fall in love with a cowboy. Apparently, she'd been a summer fling to him. Once she'd gone, she was out of sight and out of the man's mind.

Mona returned bearing a paddle with a number on it.

"What's that?" Gwen asked.

"What does it look like?" Mona held it out.

Gwen shook her head and raised her hands. "Oh no. I'm not going there."

"Yes. You are." Mona took Gwen's hand and placed the paddle in her palm. "You do have a sizeable chunk of money you really want to go to the women's shelter, don't you?"

"I'll make a donation. I don't need a date with a cowboy to do that."

"Well, the only cowboys who will be here tonight are the ones going up for bid. If you want one to help you out with Dalton, you'll have to up the ante and bid for him."

Her stomach burbled and her chest tightened. "I can't." Despite her protest, a tingle of anticipation rippled through her.

"You're a high-powered business owner with more balls than most men I know."

"Exactly." Gwen nodded, pushing aside the insane thought of owning a cowboy. "I don't need to buy a cowboy to prove it."

"Honey. Yes. You. Do." Mona curled Gwen's fingers around the paddle. "Bring on the cowboys!" she yelled. "We're gonna ride one tonight!"

Libby stood behind the bar, holding the tequila bottle up for Gwen to see. "More?"

"Yeah, I guess."

The bartender tipped the tequila into her shot glass. "Will that be all?"

Gwen rolled her eyes, her stomach pitching. "Make it a double. I think I'm buying a cowboy tonight."

ABOUT THE AUTHOR

Twenty years of livin' and lovin' on a South Texas ranch raising horses, cattle, goats, ostriches and emus left an indelible impression on Myla Jackson, one she likes to instill in her red-hot stories. Myla pens wildly sexy, fun adventures of all genres including historical westerns, medieval tales, romantic suspense, contemporary romance and paranormal beasties of all shapes and sexy sizes. or spending time with her family. She lives in the tree-covered hills of Northwest Arkansas with her husband of more than 20 years and her muses—the human-wanna-be canines—Chewy and Sweetpea.

To learn more about Myla Jackson and her alter ego Elle James visit:
www.mylajackson.com
mylajackson@mylajackson.com

Duty Bound

River Bound

Paranormal

Shewolf

Thorn's Kiss

Sex, Lies & Vampire Hunters

9 781626 951129